A POETIC BALLAD

A CROSSWORD MYSTERY

ADITYA BANERJEE

notionpress.com

INDIA • SINGAPORE • MALAYSIA

Copyright © Aditya Banerjee 2023
All Rights Reserved.

ISBN 979-8-89066-726-7

This book has been published with all efforts taken to make the material error-free after the consent of the author. However, the author and the publisher do not assume and hereby disclaim any liability to any party for any loss, damage, or disruption caused by errors or omissions, whether such errors or omissions result from negligence, accident, or any other cause.

While every effort has been made to avoid any mistake or omission, this publication is being sold on the condition and understanding that neither the author nor the publishers or printers would be liable in any manner to any person by reason of any mistake or omission in this publication or for any action taken or omitted to be taken or advice rendered or accepted on the basis of this work. For any defect in printing or binding the publishers will be liable only to replace the defective copy by another copy of this work then available.

Disclaimer: This is a work of fiction. Names, characters, business, events, and incidents are the products of the author's imagination. Any resemblance to actual persons, living or dead, or actual events is purely coincidental.

Find Aditya Banerjee on

Instagram @ https://www.instagram.com/adityabanerjeeauthor/

Facebook @ https://www.facebook.com/aditya.banerjee.author/

Also by

Aditya Banerjee

Broken Dreams: A Callipur Murder Mystery

Stolen Legacies

Death in the Walled City

One day you will just be a memory to some people. Do your best to be a good one.

— Unknown

Table of Contents

1. Introduction 9
2. Letter 12
3. Family 51
4. Professor 89
5. Crosswords 128
6. Book 166
7. Woman 217
8. Kismet 275
9. Ballad 325
10. Epilogue 365

About the Author *373*

Introduction

Our story takes place in Benares, India, in the late summer of 1980. Benares, which is also known as Varanasi, sits on the banks of the Ganges River. Like the river it straddles, the city has helped shape Indian history. Benares is one of the oldest inhabited cities in India, with a recorded history dating back to the eleventh century BC. If one were to go by the Hindu epics and scriptures, it dates back even further.

One of Benares's suburbs, Sarnath, is nestled in the confluence of the Ganges and the Varuna Rivers. Ancient buildings and structures adorn Sarnath, including the famous Ashoka Pillar, that appears as an emblem on many government buildings and national monuments. The suburb's greatest claim to fame is that Buddha reportedly spent time there teaching. It remains, to this day, one of the most revered pilgrimage sites for Buddhists all over the world.

A Poet's Ballad, A Crossword Mystery

The majestic Ganges, which weaves through the plains across the northern and eastern regions, predates all cities and civilizations that rose and thrived along its banks. Revered by the Hindus as a sacred river, it takes center stage in many stories and epics in Indian mythology. The river is also a lifeline to millions of people. Many other densely populated cities hug the banks of the Ganges besides Benares, including Haridwar, Kanpur, Patna, and Calcutta in India and Dhaka in Bangladesh. The mighty river starts in the Himalayas to the north and traverses the breadth of India and Bangladesh before reaching the Indian Ocean in the Bay of Bengal, traveling just over twenty-five hundred kilometers.

During the 1980s, India was far from the economic powerhouse it is today. Prospects for graduates, especially in humanities studies, were scarce. The most sought-after jobs were in the government and in the government-owned public-sector companies. Competition was fierce, prompting many unsuccessful aspirers to look abroad for a meaningful life and career.

The family structure in India was changing rapidly. Large, multigenerational families living under one roof were disappearing, with the younger generation leaving their hometowns for better jobs, forming more nuclear families.

The workforce was predominantly male, although women were making inroads in all sectors of the economy. In large metropolises like Delhi or Bombay, women in the workforce were increasingly common. However, the change was more gradual in smaller towns and cities.

Readers will get the sense that Benares was a much more conservative town compared with Delhi, and, to a large extent, that is a fair depiction of society at that time. It was the age of rotary phones. Most Indian households did not own a phone or TV, and the primary source of news was the newspaper.

Letter

Mahesh pressed his pillow over his ears as sharp knocks battered the door. Muffled voices and laughter rose from outside his hostel room, and the knocking grew louder. With a groan, Mahesh sat up in bed. From the level of racket, he guessed that his neighbors were gathering for their Saturday cricket match. He was about to get the door, but the memory of his dream kept him glued firmly in place.

He pushed his hair back, drawing a shaky breath. An old man had stood on the banks of the Ganges, his face obscured by shadows beneath the moonlight. When Mahesh had called out to him, the man had swung to face him, the whites of his eyes gleaming in the darkness. He'd reached out to Mahesh with a trembling hand.

"Please," the man had moaned in a haunting voice. "Help me."

Mahesh had woken up with a start, his stomach sinking as he'd tried to place where he'd heard that voice before. So familiar . . .

"Wake up, you lazy oafs!" a voice laughed through the door.

After stealing a glance at his roommate, who was still fast asleep—or at least pretending to be—Mahesh dragged his feet to the door and swung it open.

His hallmate stood smiling, a group of rowdy teammates chatting and shoving each other behind him.

"Ah, I knew you were awake! Could we borrow some water bottles and clean T-shirts for the match this morning?"

Mahesh smiled, shaking his head in exasperation. "Believe it or not, some of us actually enjoy sleeping in on the weekends. Okay, come on in." The request wasn't unusual. Neighbors in the student housing complex often shared such necessities, and he knew they'd do the same for him. As the players flooded in, grabbing what they needed, Mahesh's hallmate leaned against the doorframe.

"Hey, did you hear about that retired professor who died recently? He taught at Delhi University, and a few of my classmates knew him from before they transferred here. They are saying he passed away under mysterious circumstances."

Mahesh furrowed his brow as he dodged a scurrying cricket player. "Which professor?"

His hallmate shrugged. "I don't recall his name. There are plenty of theories going around regarding his death, but I won't bore you with rumors." As the other players scrambled out of the room, he shot Mahesh a smirk. "I'd invite you to watch the match, but I know you're not interested in cricket. I can't fathom how you can even call yourself Indian. It's downright unpatriotic!"

Mahesh chuckled. "Hey, I play sports! I love to run, and I'll remind you that I'm the reigning chess champion here at JNU."

His hostel mate rolled his eyes, grabbing a shirt and a water bottle for himself. "You can hardly call chess and running sports, but sure. Thanks again for this!"

Mahesh gave him a nod, and the players cheered and whooped as they made for the field. As Mahesh latched the door shut, he wondered which professor his neighbor had been referring to. Did Mahesh know him from his time at Delhi University? As he shuffled across the room, the passport on his desk, half hidden beneath his latest crossword puzzle, caught his eye. A smile tugged at his lips.

He had finally received his student visa to study abroad. Although the approval letter had arrived nearly three months ago, the visa process had dragged out longer than expected. Now that everything was in order, he was leaving for the United Kingdom in two weeks to pursue a PhD in history. Anxiety mixed with excitement when he thought of the upcoming journey, but he was ready.

His eyes then roved to his roommate, Bharat, whose sheet was still pulled up to his nose. Mahesh couldn't fathom the guy's ability to sleep through that ruckus. Or maybe it was a ploy to avoid answering the door. After getting dressed, he opened the curtains on his side of the room. Bharat groaned as sunlight flooded in. He let out a curse and pulled the sheet over his head. But it was too late. It was a summer morning in Delhi, after all. The dingy ceiling fan only served to circulate the same sweltering air around the tiny space.

A Poet's Ballad, A Crossword Mystery

Their room, like all university hostel rooms, barely had enough space for their belongings. Many students tucked their luggage under their beds to hold the overflow of stuff from their cramped closets.

As Bharat tossed and turned on his mattress, Mahesh braced himself for the barrage of insults coming his way. He wasn't disappointed. Bharat was known for his colorful language and used it remarkably well when he was irritated. He was a good friend, so Mahesh just brushed it off.

They'd been roommates since their undergraduate days at Delhi University, choosing to stick together while pursuing their master's degrees at Delhi's prestigious Jawaharlal Nehru University. Having just graduated, they were now preparing to set off in different directions. Mahesh was bound for the UK while Bharat would be returning to his hometown of Bhopal. Following many rounds of interviews, he had managed to secure a job at one of the public-sector companies there.

Mahesh gazed out the window as Bharat continued to grumble under his breath. The sprawling JNU campus was thinning out. Summer was usually quiet, with most students vacating their hostels by the first week of July. Bharat had decided to stay an extra three weeks to attend a wedding in Delhi, and to bid farewell to his friend who was going abroad, of course. Mahesh's heart sank at the thought. They both knew that once they went their separate ways, it would be difficult to meet up again.

"Is your whole family going to be seeing you off?" Bharat asked groggily, as if reading his mind.

"Just my parents." Mahesh swallowed hard, remembering the heated exchange they'd shared the last time they spoke. Things were tense between him and his father, but he was still eager to see them.

Bharat had put on his glasses and was now rummaging for a shirt from the pile of clothing on his desk chair. "Where are all my clean shirts?"

"The cricket players took a few."

With a grimace, Bharat smelled the remaining shirts one by one to find which would be least repulsive.

"What's wrong with you?" Bharat grumbled.

"What do you mean?"

"Why did you wake me up so early?" Bharat asked after putting on his T-shirt.

"I'm hungry."

"So?"

"I thought you'd like to join me," Mahesh said with a smile.

"Unbelievable. I shudder to think what you will subject your roommates in London to."

"Yeah, it will be tough to find someone who can sleep through a typhoon and smells like a landfill."

Bharat threw a dirty shirt at Mahesh. "All right, we ought to head to the canteen anyway. Professor Sarkar is leaving tomorrow, and this will be our last chance to see him."

"Right." Mahesh nodded.

Sarkar was an English professor at JNU, but Mahesh and Bharat knew him better as their hostel's beloved warden. His office was on the ground floor opposite the canteen and doubled as the mailroom. One wall of his spacious office featured nothing but rows of mailboxes.

Mahesh knew that this was most likely by design. Nearly all the residents hailed from outside Delhi, and they often received letters from their families. A trip to the mailroom would invariably mean a conversation with Sarkar about their well-being and any problems they were grappling with in life or school.

The canteen was nearly empty when they arrived. With the kickoff of summer break, the canteen workforce was down to a few skeleton staff.

As one of the premier cafeterias on campus, it boasted a wide assortment of menu items and, more importantly, a large sitting area both inside and outside the building. When Mahesh noticed an older man with a white beard serving up food, he recalled his strange dream. He almost brought it up to Bharat but then thought better of it. His friend was famous for conjuring elaborate theories to explain the unknown, and Mahesh wasn't in the mood.

After they picked up their egg sandwiches and tea, Mahesh stepped out to the courtyard. There, benches and picnic tables were shaded beneath a canopy of trees. Bharat followed a few steps behind, stopping and exchanging greetings with people he knew.

As Mahesh sat down and waited for Bharat, he looked around. He would miss the leafy courtyards, the sprawling campus, the canteens, and the classrooms. He hadn't given them much thought during the last two years. But now that he was leaving, he viewed them with a sense of belonging and nostalgia. The loud thud of a tray hitting the table jarred him from his reverie.

"Did we lose you somewhere?" Bharat asked, sitting across from Mahesh.

"You know, I am going to miss this place."

"I won't," Bharat scoffed, taking a big bite of his sandwich.

"Maybe I'm just feeling sentimental because I'm leaving the country."

"It's a good thing that you are."

"What do you mean?"

"Don't get me wrong, I will miss you dearly. But honestly, there isn't much for you in India."

"You really think so?" Mahesh asked between sips of tea.

"My friend, this is 1980. There aren't enough jobs for science graduates, let alone folks pursuing the arts. If you weren't going abroad, you would have only two choices."

"And what are they?" Mahesh asked, slightly amused.

"You either take the civil services exam to get a government job, or you earn a PhD and become a professor somewhere. Of course, in your case, you could join the family business, but I don't see you selling clothes. Come to think of it, a government job is really not an option for you either."

Mahesh narrowed his eyes. "Really? Why not?"

"Look at how many people take the civil services exam and the number who get in. It's almost impossible. You may be smart, but you are not studious or disciplined enough to make the cut."

"I appreciate your confidence in my abilities," Mahesh said while nibbling on his sandwich. "What about the second option?"

"Doing a PhD here in India? That's a horrible route. The student stipends are lower than the wages of the university cleaning staff, and when you do get your degree, you are looking at salaries that are hardly enough to live on," Bharat responded as he finished off his sandwich.

"I know you're right, but it's not that straightforward. Even though I put my foot down about going abroad, there's a part of me that's scared. What if it doesn't work out?"

"Well, you could always come back to India and try your luck here. For all you know, a degree from abroad might help you get a better academic position."

"Yeah, it might, but . . ." Mahesh trailed off with a sigh, cringing at the thought of facing his family should he fail at his endeavors abroad—especially considering how things went down.

When Mahesh had first secured his admission in the UK, his father had been furious, wanting Mahesh to stay back and join their family's textile business. Eventually, Mahesh had won the argument. But his father had made it clear that any hope of him joining the family business upon his return was now remote.

Mahesh had readily agreed. His siblings didn't object either—they were probably relieved. It meant more shares of their modest business to go around. But Mahesh had certainly caused some waves in the family.

Bharat's voice drew him out of his thoughts. "What's bothering you?"

"It's how things ended with my father. He wasn't just angry. He was disappointed. I was angry too, and we both said a lot of things in the heat of the moment. Plus, if my foray abroad doesn't work out, there would be a lot of snide remarks from my siblings."

"Then you will just have to prove them wrong, won't you?"

Just as Mahesh opened his mouth to reply, he heard footsteps. They both looked sideways to see Professor Sarkar ambling toward their table. They immediately got up and offered him a seat. He smiled and gestured that they should sit. Once they all settled in, Mahesh asked whether he would like something from the cafeteria.

"Oh no. I really shouldn't. My doctor told me to cut down on my intake of tea and snacks. You know, when I was in my forties, he asked me to quit smoking, and I tried. Now, in my late fifties, he is asking me to quit all kinds of food. Have you noticed that these doctors always tell you to cut out the delicious stuff and not the bland fare like vegetables?"

"I agree, sir. It's a conspiracy. They don't want us to have a happy life," Bharat responded with a smirk.

"Exactly," the professor said before turning to Mahesh. "Anyway, I am not here to talk about myself. Mahesh, are you all set for your next adventure in London?"

"Yes, sir," Mahesh replied, excitement lacing his tone.

"Which university did you end up with, again?"

"UCL."

"Ah, University College London. I am guessing you chose it based on the supervisor and what your professors recommended."

"That, and also funding, sir," Mahesh said.

Sarkar arched his eyebrows. "You are getting a better stipend?"

"That's right. Plus, the tuition is lower than that of Oxford or Cambridge. They are also helping me with housing, and if I share with other students, I will come out ahead even though London is quite expensive."

"Well, I am sure you have done the math. I am happy for you. When are you leaving?"

"In two weeks," Mahesh responded.

"Time flies, doesn't it? I am heading to Calcutta for summer break, and I don't think I'll be seeing either of you for a while," Sarkar said with a smile, glancing between Mahesh and Bharat.

"I will certainly write, sir," Mahesh replied, knowing full well that once he was in London, it would be difficult to keep in touch with everyone.

"Oh, please do." Sarkar shifted, as if preparing to leave. "I love receiving letters from my former students. Oh, before I forget, you have a letter in the mailbox from Benares, Mahesh."

"I will pass by and pick it up. Thank you for letting me know."

"Off to do my packing, then. Good luck to both of you in all your future endeavors. I hope you do well, and remember—it's never as good or as bad as it seems. Take it from an old man. Enjoy the little things, and stay true to yourself. Try to make a difference if you can. There isn't time for anything else." Sarkar gave them one last smile as he turned to leave.

"Thank you, sir," Mahesh and Bharat replied in unison.

After Sarkar left, a few classmates stopped by to wish Mahesh well on his new adventure as he and Bharat finished their masala tea.

When the last classmate left, Bharat shot Mahesh a snarky smile. "See? Now you're the star attraction simply because you are leaving India to study abroad. You've become such a hotshot."

"Jealous, are we?" Mahesh teased.

"Totally." Bharat laughed. "So, what's with the letter from Benares? Do you think it's Karan?"

"Must be. I don't know anyone else there," Mahesh responded, feeling a prick of curiosity.

Karan was a friend from their undergraduate days at Delhi University. They'd all hailed from out of town, so after the first year of college, they'd rented an apartment together. While Mahesh and Bharat moved on to JNU after graduation, Karan returned to his hometown of Benares to take charge of the family's hospitality business. They tried to stay in touch, but over time, they had drifted apart. Then, six months ago, Bharat and Mahesh received an invitation to Karan's wedding in Benares.

Like most traditional Indian weddings, it had been an elaborate affair. Fortunately, Karan had managed to carve out some time to spend with Bharat and Mahesh despite the madness surrounding all the ceremonies. During those few hours together, they'd felt like they were back in college again. After that, there hadn't been any other correspondence besides the occasional cards during festivals.

"Well, let's check out that letter," Bharat said, getting up.

"Yeah. Maybe he is having a kid or something."

"Or maybe his wife ran away, and he is finally free," Bharat blurted gleefully.

"Honestly, Bharat, I sometimes wonder what goes on inside that head of yours," Mahesh said with a smile.

"It's definitely one of the unexplored wonders of the world."

It was a short walk from the cafeteria to the mailboxes at Sarkar's office. The usual hustle and bustle of the hostel had given way to a more laid-back atmosphere. Some students had piled their luggage in the courtyard just outside the main entrance, waiting for their rides to the railway station or airport. The building housed nearly three hundred students, most of whom had already left for summer break.

Stepping into the mailroom, Mahesh quickly emptied his mailbox. There were a few flyers and then the letter from Benares. Mahesh scrunched his eyebrows in confusion. It was not from Karan, but from a gentleman whose name he didn't recognize. Mahesh showed the sender's address to Bharat, who shrugged.

"I don't know who this is," Mahesh said, still sorting through his confusion.

"There's only one way to find out."

Mahesh carefully opened the envelope, making sure not to rip anything that was written on it. A single sheet of paper lay folded inside. The letter was handwritten in an exquisite script, but the message itself was short.

Mahesh's mouth went dry as he scanned the letter. Devesh Tripathi, a retired professor who'd taught at Delhi University, had passed away a few weeks ago. He'd left a box with Mahesh's name on it, along with some papers and books. As for the box, the writer, Hari Das, gave no details of the contents.

Mahesh lowered the inscribed paper. This had to be the professor his hallmate had mentioned. Since the letter contained nothing personal or confidential, Mahesh handed it to Bharat.

His friend took his time reading it and then handed it back to Mahesh. "This gentleman, Hari, was a friend of Professor Devesh Tripathi?"

"That's what it seems." Mahesh read the letter once more, this time slowly and carefully.

"I remember that guy, Devesh. Wasn't he the fellow who ran the magazine and was crazy about crossword puzzles?"

Mahesh nodded. "One and the same."

"I didn't think you knew him that well."

"We weren't very close, but I did interact with him for magazine-related things during our undergraduate studies. But since he taught biology, I never had any classes with him."

Devesh had run the monthly magazine flawlessly, making sure that funds were allocated for printing, the editorial board gave their blessing on the content, and the monthly editions were published in a timely manner.

The one section of the publication that Devesh had personally labored over was the crossword puzzle. The man had loved creating and solving them. He would spend hours putting together two elaborate puzzles for each edition. Mahesh had shared Devesh's enthusiasm for crossword puzzles, and they would often pick up papers and journals to solve them together.

Bharat locked eyes with Mahesh. "Strange that someone would contact you on his passing."

"Well . . . " Mahesh started, but he was interrupted by Bharat.

"As I recall, we *did* see Devesh briefly at Karan's wedding. He looked different from when we knew him during our days at DU."

"You're right. He was more subdued, and he seemed exhausted, frail even," Mahesh remarked.

"Do you think he was ill at that time?" Bharat wondered.

"I don't know. I spoke to him for a moment, and then he went home with his nephew." Mahesh hadn't wanted to pry into his affairs. Inquiring about one's health could be sensitive. "I remember that he left early. It is rather strange that he would leave a box for me, though."

"Well, there are a few numbers here. We can call those to find out more. This doesn't look like a hoax to me," Bharat said, gesturing to the letter.

"I agree," Mahesh mumbled.

"The letter asks that you pick up the box in person, which seems a bit much. You could always ask this gentleman, Hari Das, to mail the contents to you."

A Poet's Ballad, A Crossword Mystery

"I suppose I could, but the tone of the letter is rather insistent that I retrieve it in person. Don't you think that's a strange request?"

"All this is extremely weird," Bharat said. "Maybe he left you some secret treasure or hidden wealth or tons of money."

"Enough. Really, Bharat," Mahesh said, casting him a glare. The letter contained nothing to suggest any sort of windfall for the recipient. But then, why leave him anything in the first place? As they both sat down to ponder their next move, Mahesh recalled his time with the professor.

Devesh hailed from Benares and was unmarried. After retiring, the same year Mahesh finished his BA, Devesh had moved back to his hometown. Word was that he had gone to live in the small ancestral home that he shared with his nephew and his nephew's wife. After that, they had never heard from Devesh again, which was not unusual. Mahesh figured that if indeed Devesh were to keep in touch with any of his students, it would be those he had taught.

When they ran into him at Karan's wedding, Devesh had said something about recovering from an accident or a fall that had happened a few months earlier. The last thing Mahesh remembered was the professor being helped by his nephew toward the exit of the reception hall. He had turned around and waved at them with a sad smile.

"I think we should give this Hari Das a call," Bharat said finally.

Mahesh nodded. "Yes, let's do that."

"Are you seriously considering going to Benares?"

"Based on this, no. Let me talk to his friend and then his nephew. I can decide after that."

"Yeah, makes sense. At least they can tell you what's in the box and whether they can just mail it to you."

"That's what I'm thinking," Mahesh said, feeling unsure.

"You still have two weeks till you leave for London. You could always go there and come back. You could meet up with Karan and stay at one of his family's guesthouses, or maybe he could put you up at his home."

"That's true, though I'd prefer the guesthouse option. They live in a large joint family, and if I stayed at his place, I would constantly be dealing with people. The guesthouse would be good for Karan too. That way, we could talk more freely."

"Yes, there's that." Bharat stroked his chin in thought. "Do you want to call from my uncle's travel agency? It will be cheaper, and if you decide to go, you can buy your railway ticket from there at a discount."

"You think of everything, don't you?" Mahesh asked with a grin.

"It sucks that I won't be able to go with you. Even if this amounts to nothing, I'd have loved to meet up with Karan and do some sightseeing in Benares. But I can't skip my cousin's wedding, especially with my parents here."

"I understand. Don't worry. If I decide to go, it won't be for more than a week."

"All right. Let's get moving then," Bharat said.

They exited into the courtyard, where they saw a few taxis parked out front. Mahesh and Bharat stepped onto the road leading out of the JNU campus. Although the weather was sweltering, the canopy of trees lining the street provided ample shade.

Leaving the sprawling campus, they headed for the nearest bus stop. They didn't have to wait long and were soon on their way to Delhi's South Extension Market.

Figuring he'd reread the letter while they rode, Mahesh dug into his shoulder bag. But instead, his fingers brushed the corner of another paper. He pulled it out and realized it was a crossword puzzle. Funny. He didn't remember ever starting this one. As he scanned the puzzle, his eyes fell on number seven, across. A four-letter word for the inevitable future. After thinking for a moment, he smiled as he penned in the answer. *Fate*.

Tucking the puzzle back into his bag, he let his mind wander to Devesh Tripathi.

"Did you know Devesh was an amateur poet?" he declared after a short while.

"No, I wasn't aware," Bharat said and leaned back in his seat.

"He never published anything in the college magazine. The rest of the students and staff often wondered why. Some of us asked him, but he was always coy with his responses."

"Did he share them with anyone? Like, did anyone actually read his stuff?"

"Not that I recall. He told us that he used to go to these poetry festivals. You know, Kavi Sammelans. Maybe he recited something there," Mahesh replied.

Bharat shook his head in disbelief. "As I said, I still find it strange that he would ask someone to contact you after he died."

"I agree, especially since we were never that close."

"Well, I mean . . . from what we know, he was a bit off."

"How so?" Mahesh was curious, knowing full well that Bharat would concoct some strange, convoluted theory.

"Think about it. He was a single biology professor who wrote poetry and was crazy about crossword puzzles. Any one of those things probably isn't a red flag, but taken together, it feels a bit eccentric."

Mahesh chuckled. "It's a good thing you are not studying psychology. I don't think any of that is weird."

"Or maybe his poems were just so bad that he didn't want to share them with anyone."

"Honestly, Bharat. The guy is dead. Show some respect."

"I am. I'm only talking about his poetry, not him."

"The letter doesn't mention how he passed away," Mahesh said, remembering his hallmate saying something about mysterious circumstances.

"Well, all I know is that he really, *really* loved those crossword puzzles, and you were also into them. Weren't you part of a club or something?"

"Yes, the Lexico club. Lexico was the original name for Scrabble," replied Mahesh, "and Devesh always shared tips and tricks to play the game and solve puzzles."

"And as far as you know, that's the only thing you had in common?"

"That's all I can think of," Mahesh said. He turned to gaze out the window. The summer sun was piercing through the glass, making for an uncomfortable bus ride. Luckily, it wasn't long before they got off at one of the main intersections of the market. Their destination was a short walk from there.

Bharat's uncle ran a successful travel agency, garnering a lot of business from students and their families from out of town. He didn't seem to mind his nephew's occasional requests to let his friends make calls. Long-distance rates were high between cities in India, and students were always on a tight budget. Mahesh had met the man quite a few times. Apart from some annoying habits, such as chewing tobacco and lecturing anyone who disagreed with him on politics and cricket, they got along well.

When they arrived, a few agents were busy attending to clients, and Bharat's uncle was barking away on the phone behind a wide desk at the far end of the store. The air-conditioned office was a welcome respite from the heat outside.

Upon spotting his nephew and Mahesh, the old man waved them over and pointed to the chairs across his desk. After he hung up, he gave them a warm smile. He had a small, round stature beneath a balding head, but his stoic expression hid a man with a big heart who lavished his family and friends with gifts during Diwali. Though a shrewd businessman, he was generous with his wealth and donated to many charities. Bharat often wondered aloud to Mahesh whether this was a ploy to eventually enter politics.

"How are things going with you two? Ready for your summer break?"

"Yes, uncle," Bharat and Mahesh responded, their voices overlapping.

They talked briefly about JNU and Mahesh's trip to London for higher studies before guiding the conversation to the purpose of their visit. One of the staff brought them some lassis and samosas. Before letting Mahesh use the phone, Bharat's uncle gave him a long lecture on how he should conduct himself in London, how to go about seeing the town, and the various pitfalls of Western culture. Mahesh listened intently without arguing. After a few minutes, he retreated to a small desk with a phone to make the calls to Benares. Meanwhile, Bharat kept his uncle occupied with never-ending discussions about Bollywood and an upcoming cricket series between India and the West Indies.

Mahesh's first call was to Hari Das, the man who had sent him the letter. Hari picked up after a few rings, and Mahesh introduced himself.

"Yes, I was expecting your call, and I am glad you contacted me," Hari said. His voice sounded like that of an older gentleman.

"Sir, can you tell me anything about the contents of the box that the professor left for me?"

"Unfortunately, I can't. Devesh's only instructions, written in a letter to me, were to notify you to pick up something he has left for you," Hari said.

"Oh. Is there anything else pertaining to me in the letter?"

"It just states that you should pick up the box, and he would appreciate it if you did so in person," Hari said before letting a silence stretch between them.

"Where is the box now?" Mahesh asked.

"With his nephew, Laxman, who he was living with," Hari huffed, and Mahesh detected a sharp change in his tone. "You must collect it from him soon. I don't think he is going to keep it for too long."

"His nephew didn't share the details of the contents with you?"

"No, he told me that the box was meant for you, and he would hand it over *only* to you. He also said that if no one came to collect the box, he would just throw it away. That guy is a piece of work! I never liked him. He never took care of Devesh properly," Hari grumbled with a tinge of disgust.

Mahesh tried to move the conversation along. "If I do come to Benares, can I visit you?" he asked.

"What do you mean 'if'? Devesh left this for you. You *must* come and pick it up. His students were all he had, and this was important to him!" Hari boomed.

Mahesh was taken aback, but Hari and Devesh had obviously been close friends. It was natural for Hari to defend his dying wish.

"I'll be there on Monday, sir," Mahesh said. "I will come by your place after I have settled in."

"Do you have a place to stay in Benares? If not, you can stay with me."

Mahesh was again surprised, this time pleasantly. "Thank you, but I have a friend who lives there. I will see if I can stay with him. If I need your help, I will certainly ask."

"Please do, and I look forward to seeing you on Monday. Have a safe trip."

"Thank you," Mahesh said before hanging up.

He had wanted to ask more about how Devesh had died, but he was wary of extending his conversation as Bharat's uncle was keeping an eye on him.

Mahesh brought out a little notebook where he had written Karan's number. Luckily, it was Karan who picked up. Mahesh quickly told him that he would be taking the overnight train on Sunday and would be in Benares for a few days. Karan gave him the address and the street number of the guesthouse where he could stay, adding that he would pick him up at the railway station on Monday morning.

After hanging up, Mahesh felt a swell of relief. He glanced back down at the letter, finding the second phone number, the one belonging to Laxman Tripathi. He dialed, but there was no answer. Mahesh put down the receiver and headed back to where Bharat and his uncle were seated.

After he quickly relayed what had happened, Bharat's uncle called an agent over to take down Mahesh's details. He then instructed the agent to book a train ticket for Sunday night from Delhi to Benares. While the agent was busy making the reservation and Bharat's uncle was on the phone with some tour operators, Bharat pointed Mahesh to a desk a little farther away where they could talk in private.

"It's a good thing you are going. You and Karan can have some fun, even if this box turns out to be useless. I am just jealous that I can't be with you guys," Bharat said, finishing off his lassi with a long sip.

"It would have been nice to reach the nephew, Laxman, as well."

"Well, you can give it another shot before we leave."

"Yes. I must thank your uncle."

"And you should thank me too. Had you not known me, you wouldn't have met my uncle."

"Right. How could I ever forget?" Mahesh said with a smile before adding, "thank you."

"Oh, don't worry. Even if you forget, I will remind you," Bharat said, and they both broke into laughter.

A moment later, the agent who had made the train reservation came over. He handed the ticket and details to Mahesh, who gave him the required payment. The ticket wasn't expensive, and he had purchased a nonrefundable, second-class sleeper berth. He checked the booking to ensure everything was in order and then headed over to Bharat's uncle's desk. Mahesh thanked him profusely, and once again, the man offered Mahesh some unsolicited advice on the pros and cons of living abroad. Thankfully, his phone started ringing, and once he returned to his customers, Bharat managed to whisk Mahesh toward the exit. His uncle waved them goodbye from afar, now back to bellowing orders on the phone and to everyone around him.

"Do you want to give Devesh's nephew another go?" Bharat asked.

"I'm not sure. I am going there anyway. I just wanted to make sure that Laxman will be there when I stop by to pick up the box, that's all."

"Go ahead then," Bharat said, pointing to the phone on the desk nearest them.

"I think we should ask your uncle again."

"Make the call, and I will go ask him. Don't worry about it." Bharat hustled over to his uncle's desk. From their body language, Mahesh gathered that Bharat's uncle didn't mind and was more preoccupied with the agents huddled around his desk.

Mahesh quickly dialed the number. A woman picked up on the other end.

"I am trying to reach Mr. Laxman Tripathi. My name is Mahesh Pal, and I believe there is a box in my name from Professor Devesh Tripathi."

"Oh yes," the woman replied. "Laxman is not here at the moment. I am his wife, Rani. We can send the box over to you. You live in Delhi, right?"

"That's right," Mahesh replied, "but I have booked myself a trip to Benares and will be arriving on Monday. I can pick up the box in person."

"Oh," Rani replied. Mahesh couldn't make out whether there was a shade of disappointment in her voice.

"Mrs. Tripathi, I will be staying with a friend for a few days. If you are going to be there on Monday, I can come by and pick up the box," Mahesh said.

He could hear some noise in the background, and then, after a brief pause, Rani spoke again. "My husband just returned home. You can speak to him now."

Then, another voice, serious and demanding, said, "This is Laxman Tripathi."

Mahesh again politely explained his plans. As he spoke, he was met with complete silence on the other end. When he finished, there was a brief pause before Laxman replied, "So, I see you have spoken to Hari Das."

"Yes, sir. He is the one who wrote to me about the box."

"Of course," Laxman sneered, "my uncle's so-called friend."

Mahesh was at a loss for words. After a moment, he decided to break the silence. "Is it okay, sir, if I pass by on Monday to pick up the box?"

"Sure, why not? Come by. You really shouldn't have to come all this way. We could have just sent you the box. There's really nothing in it—some newspaper cuttings of sports events and crossword puzzles. It's useless stuff that my uncle used to dabble in."

"Right." Mahesh noted that Laxman's voice was now much calmer and more subdued.

"What time will you be coming?"

"My train arrives in the morning. I could be there in the afternoon or evening, whichever works best for you, sir."

"It has to be evening, after six. I should be back from work by then," Laxman confirmed.

"Certainly. I will come by after six, then."

"Do you have our address? Did Hari include it in his letter?"

"Yes," Mahesh replied.

"It's a wasted visit. Your choice, though. Rani tells me that you are visiting a friend. Well, if you were going to be in Benares anyway, then yeah, it makes sense to collect it in person."

"Thank you, sir. I will see you on Monday evening."

After hanging up, Mahesh suddenly felt tired. But at the same time, the conversation had left him intrigued.

Bharat had meandered back to where he was sitting. "How did it go?"

"Strange," Mahesh said softly, his voice trailing off.

"How so?"

"It almost seemed that this guy didn't want me to come to his place to pick up the box. He was fine mailing it to me, though."

"Weird. Did he tell you what's in it?" Bharat asked.

"That's the other thing. It seems he has gone through the contents. From what he said, it's mostly newspaper cuttings and crossword puzzles."

"Wow, is that what you are going all the way to Benares for? To pick up this sort of junk?"

"I'm not sure. I have a feeling there's more to it than that."

"Well, you can tell me all the gory details on the bus back to JNU. Let's get out of this place," Bharat said as they approached the door.

"Sure." Mahesh nodded and turned to Bharat's uncle, waving to him once again before exiting the office.

On the bus ride back, Mahesh relayed to Bharat in great detail his short conversations with Hari Das and Laxman Tripathi. For once, Bharat gave Mahesh his full attention without interrupting.

When he finished, Bharat nodded slowly. "We're clearly missing something. Either way, I think going to Benares to pick up the box is the right decision."

Mahesh hummed his agreement, but as the bus rolled along, he had an uneasy feeling in the pit of his stomach. Something in the tone of those brief phone conversations didn't sit right. He just couldn't put a finger on it. Although it was nearly forty-five degrees Celsius outside, Mahesh felt a chill crawl up his spine.

Family

Aarvi Lal was happy to be back managing her father's bookshop. She had taken a week off to overlook the preparations for her upcoming wedding with Jeev. They were getting married in two weeks, and they had finally completed most of the arrangements. The week off had helped. She had spent almost the entire week with her mother, her aunts, and her soon-to-be mother-in-law, picking out sarees, jewelry, and other essentials for the wedding.

Six days of intense shopping had finally come to an end. Initially, she had enjoyed the time off, but toward the end of the week, she had grown weary of the discussions, arguments, bickering, and bargaining.

She was looking forward to her married life with Jeev and becoming Mrs. Kumar. The Lal and Kumar families had known each other for generations. But the preparations and all the events leading up to the actual wedding, not to mention dealing with her family, had made Aarvi want to run away and elope.

When she arrived at the Sanskriti Bookshop on Sunday morning, she was greeted by the lone employee who had come in early to open the store.

The bookstore stood a few blocks away from Assi Ghat, the southernmost ghat in Benares, a popular hangout for tourists throughout the year and pilgrims during festivals and ceremonies. There were many guesthouses in the area, which meant a constant stream of visitors to the ghat for recreational and cultural activities. A few yoga schools had popped up nearby, and this morning, Aarvi had seen people near the ghat doing yoga. As was the case with most ghats in Benares, there were also boats offering rides along the Ganges. Aarvi could see a few people already on the boats, heading out for their excursions.

Another thing that brought traffic to the bookstore was the nearby Benares Hindu University. A number of students frequented the bookshop, and it had become a popular hangout. Most of the store's business came from tourists and students.

A few years ago, Aarvi had convinced her father, Tarun Lal, to open a small tea stall adjacent to the bookshop and cordon off a section of the large store for used books. Initially, he had resisted. But he eventually had relented, more to pacify his daughter than anything else. These two changes had led to an uptick in sales, and business was good.

The Sanskriti Bookshop was the largest one in Benares. Founded by Aarvi's great-grandfather before India's independence, it had grown in size and business with each passing generation. The two-story building featured a large hall on the ground floor stacked with racks of books on each wall and aisles in the center. They sold books of all kinds—fiction, nonfiction, tourist guides, textbooks, and reference books. Toward the far end of the store was a small section where they sold maps, notebooks, water bottles, bags, and other accessories. One item that was slowly gaining traction was film for cameras.

The upper floor was divided into three sections. One was a large storage room for supplies. Another section had small cubicles that acted as offices for employees, equipped with a few desks, chairs, and typewriters. The third section was usually off-limits. It featured shelves of rare books that the family had collected over the years, mostly written in Sanskrit, Hindi, and Bengali. Many of them were first editions and were kept behind closed doors.

The store hosted an annual event during which authors and dignitaries were invited to see this collection, and some books were auctioned off to raise money for charity or reinvesting in the bookshop. Many tourists had heard about these rare books, so Tarun opened this section to the public once a month on an invitation-only basis to display them.

The bookshop also published a small monthly newsletter. It was usually a five or six pages bound in a thin journal with a cover showcasing the bookshop and Assi Ghat. Apart from the occasional flyers that Aarvi's father took out in newspapers during festivals, this humble newsletter served as their only advertising. The content was primarily events happening in and around Assi Ghat, new additions to the bookstore, services for tourists and students in the area, and ads for guesthouses. The intent of the publication was to drive foot traffic through and around the area, which would invariably mean a visit to the bookstore.

For the most part, the journal paid for itself. Businesses in the area were happy to have their establishments advertised. It was a much cheaper option than going to a national or regional newspaper. Tarun had the monthly journal published in a small local printing press and then had it distributed to hotels and guesthouses all over Benares.

The only content in the journal that was completely unrelated was on the back page—a crossword puzzle. One of Tarun's classmates from university had insisted that he include one in the publication, which might encourage readers to hold on to it longer and page through it more than once. Although Tarun had not been convinced, he hadn't minded including it for the sake of his friend, Devesh Tripathi. However, now that Devesh had passed away, Tarun didn't know what to do with that section.

Aarvi loved spending time at the bookshop. She loved to read and adored being around books, something she would miss once she was married. Her younger brother, Ashish, was still in high school, and it would be a few years before he could start helping their father. That worried Aarvi. Tarun was not in the best of health and had already suffered a heart attack a few years ago. The stress of running a successful establishment, his constant travels, and the long hours had taken their toll. Things were better since Aarvi had started coming to the shop, having taken over many of the responsibilities from her father. He could now come in late, leave early, and take at least one day off during the weekend.

Like his daughter, Tarun loved being surrounded by books and could spend hours talking to customers about them. He valued his collection of first editions and was proud that the store carried a wide array of books in many languages. Aarvi knew he was happy that she was getting married, but a part of her was also sad that she wouldn't be spending time with her father at the bookshop. Ashish, on the other hand, had shown no interest in the store.

The two children differed in nature and personality. Aarvi had always been a good student. She had just finished her bachelor's degree in English literature, and she had pleaded with her parents to hold off on her marriage to Jeev until she had finished her degree.

Her would-be in-laws had also agreed. She knew it was Jeev who had stepped in and convinced both sets of parents.

Ashish rarely showed up and had never really liked books. He wasn't that studious, and his only interests were cricket and photography. Tarun often worried whether he would secure enough good grades to get into a decent university. However, Ashish was still young, and his parents and sister were hopeful that he would turn things around.

Aarvi settled in behind the large desk near the store's entrance, next to the cash registers. The two clerks working the registers had come in for the day, and one of the workers had brought her some tea. With the shutters and doors finally wide open, a few tourists started trickling in, most just browsing the books and souvenirs in the traveler's section. Aarvi, meanwhile, stared down at a huge stack of papers in front of her. They included sales records from the past week and content for the monthly journal.

Aarvi had two other passions—writing short stories and doing crossword puzzles. She had been the president of the Scrabble club in her university and was proud that, during those three years, she had won the championship each time. Her interest in crossword puzzles had started when some tourists had visited the store and given her magazines and journals that featured puzzles from the weekend editions of *The New York Times*. The challenging word puzzles had piqued her interest, and she had begun scrounging every newspaper, national and regional, to solve any crosswords she could get her hands on.

Working in the bookstore helped. They carried almost all the current-affairs magazines and newspapers, and Aarvi would set aside a few copies for herself to solve the crossword puzzles. Jeev was convinced that this was an addiction. Her passion for crosswords was a solitary pursuit—that was, until her father's friend Devesh Tripathi had retired and moved back to Benares.

Devesh and Aarvi had convinced Tarun to include a crossword in the monthly newsletter. During the first year following his return to Benares, Devesh would come to the store and sit down with Aarvi to put together puzzles. But then there was the accident. It was an unfortunate hit-and-run that had left Devesh with permanent injuries. After returning from the hospital, he had been confined to his residence, and he had never fully recovered. During that time, he had sent the puzzles by mail, or his nephew, Laxman, would call the store to have someone pick them up.

Tarun and Aarvi had briefly visited Devesh a few times after the accident, but he hadn't been the same. His nephew had insisted that Devesh be given time to recover, and Tarun and Aarvi had taken this as a cue to curtail their visits. Devesh had also stopped calling, and their only correspondence with him, apart from the monthly submission of the crossword, had been the cards sent during festivals. Aarvi's upcoming wedding had also played a part in her reduced interactions with Devesh. Then came the news of Devesh's death a few weeks ago. Tarun and Aarvi had gone to the prayer ceremony to offer their condolences to the family, regretting that they hadn't done more to keep in touch with the late professor.

Aarvi was sifting through the papers on the desk when she noticed her father. Tarun was talking to one of the employees outside to make sure that the storefront looked clean and tidy. He was very big on cleanliness and aesthetics. He often got annoyed if things were out of place or if any area of the store was not cleaned properly.

It amused Aarvi immensely that her father could hardly get a word in at home when her mother left things disorganized or unkempt, but in the store, Tarun was very particular.

He slowly made his way to the desk and settled into his chair next to Aarvi. After surveying the rows of bookshelves and racks in the aisles, he turned to his daughter.

"Anything that I need to take a look at?" Tarun asked, pointing to the stack of papers that Aarvi was poring over.

"Not really. I will take care of it."

"You left early. When I woke up, your mother told me that you had already left."

"Yes, I was up early and figured I'd get started on the paperwork," Aarvi said.

"Is there any shopping left to do for the wedding? We haven't spoken much this past week."

"I know, and I missed coming to the store, too. I thought I liked shopping, but last week gave me a different perspective," Aarvi declared thoughtfully, fidgeting with her pen.

"Well, at least it's all done, right?"

"More or less. I've left the rest to Mom. I can't deal with it anymore. All these chores and arrangements take the fun out of the wedding. Maybe Jeev and I should have just run away, gotten married somewhere, and come back," Aarvi huffed.

This brought a smile to her father's face. "Well, my dear, you are our only daughter, and we have to let your mom have her way when it comes to this."

This and everything else, Aarvi thought. Unlike her father, Aarvi's mother, Ritika, was constantly on her case about every detail surrounding the wedding. She also wasn't happy with Aarvi spending so much time at the store instead of helping her. That had led to a huge argument a month ago, and her dad had had to step in to offer a compromise in which Aarvi would take a week off.

Aarvi picked up a paper from the stack and turned to Tarun. "What do we do with this?"

"What is it?" Tarun asked, searching for his glasses. Aarvi helped him locate them in his pocket.

"The crossword. We don't have Devesh Uncle anymore."

"Ah yes." Tarun sighed, his eyes downcast. "I will miss him, you know. I feel bad that I didn't do more to keep in touch with him after his accident. He still managed to send the crosswords each month."

"That's true. He is the only one I knew who liked them as much as I do."

"I guess we can remove them for now. We will fill up the section with other ads or just completely remove a page."

"Sure," Aarvi agreed.

"Oh, that reminds me—I got a call from Hari. Do you remember him? Hari Das? We have met him a few times at some functions. He was close to Devesh and was one of our batchmates."

"Yes, of course, your eccentric friend from college. I haven't spoken to him lately. I heard that everyone seems to avoid him."

"Careful, now. I am getting old too, and soon people might be calling *me* a crazy, old man."

"There's no chance of that. You are already there," Aarvi said with a smirk.

"Really?" Tarun laughed.

"Anyway, what does Hari Uncle have to do with Devesh Uncle or me?"

"Well, it seems Devesh asked him to get in touch with you to pick up some papers or something."

"That's strange. Why wouldn't Devesh Uncle or Laxman or Rani call me directly?"

"I asked him, and all he knew was that while Laxman and Rani were going through Devesh's papers, they found something with your name on it. Devesh also wrote a note to Hari stating that he'd left something for you. Why don't you go see Hari tomorrow and ask him yourself? He doesn't live far from here. Give him a call, and he can probably give you more details."

"Don't you find that odd?" Aarvi asked.

"What?"

"It almost seems as if Devesh Uncle knew he was going to die and left stuff for me," said Aarvi.

She wondered if her father also found it strange that Devesh would leave something for her and not him.

"He wasn't doing well, you know. From what Hari told me, it's not just you. Apparently, he left books and other belongings for his students as well."

"What do you think it is?" Aarvi wondered aloud.

"What do you mean?" Tarun tilted his head.

"What Devesh Uncle left for me?"

"Oh, it's probably some books and crosswords. I think you are the only one who appreciated his passion for those puzzles," Tarun remarked.

"That must be it. I will give Hari Uncle a call and meet him tomorrow. It's strange that Laxman didn't let us know. We saw him a couple of times during the prayer ceremonies, but he didn't mention anything. Neither did Rani," Aarvi said and looked away toward the store entrance. A few customers were trickling in.

"They were probably too busy to worry about all that. Or maybe they found out only while going through Devesh's papers afterward. Who knows?"

"You're right," Aarvi murmured, slowly turning her head to face her father, her mind swimming with questions.

"Something on your mind?" Tarun asked.

"I find Laxman and Rani a bit odd."

"How so?"

"I can't say for sure. It almost seemed like they didn't want Devesh Uncle to talk to us directly or come to our store often. After the accident, whenever we saw Devesh Uncle, they were always with him. Wherever he went, they seemed to be close by, guarding him. Before the accident, Devesh Uncle was cheerful and happy. After that, he suddenly became quiet, almost sad," Aarvi professed thoughtfully.

"There may be a simpler explanation for that. His mobility was restricted. Perhaps Laxman and Rani were just taking good care of him. Devesh really couldn't go anywhere on his own after what happened," Tarun declared.

"Maybe," Aarvi said. She wasn't satisfied with his response, but she didn't want to press him further.

A Poet's Ballad, A Crossword Mystery

She spent the rest of the morning at the store going through all the paperwork, getting documents approved and signed by her father, and making sure that the staff were aware of the schedule during the summer months. The shop sometimes had to hire temporary workers for a few weeks when some of their regular employees left for their annual break. It wasn't difficult to find part-time or temporary workers. There were always students in the area who were happy to gain experience working at the store.

With the documents sorted, Aarvi turned her attention to the monthly newsletter. Most of the content had already been finalized. She glanced at the folder where she kept all of Devesh's crosswords from previous editions. Sometimes he had submitted an extra one in case there was space to squeeze it in. What had the late professor left for her? She knew he was an avid reader, an amateur poet, and a fan of crosswords.

Unable to stave off her curiosity, she picked up the phone to call Hari Das. It was a short conversation, as he was busy with some guests. They agreed to meet the next day. Hari's house was a fifteen-minute walk from the bookstore, and Aarvi decided to stop by after lunch on Monday.

The rest of the day was relatively quiet. There was a constant stream of visitors, mostly tourists. Tarun was busy talking to some of them about the history of the city. She had often spoken to her father about not imposing himself on customers and engaging them in lengthy conversations. It didn't help. But part of her liked seeing him so happy just being at the store.

After Tarun's heart attack, Aarvi had taken over most of the day-to-day affairs. She had been lucky that the university was nearby, and she had been able to spend time at the store in between classes or during breaks. Now that she had graduated and was getting married, she worried that her father would once again have to bear the stress of running the store. She had trained one of the longtime employees to take over some of the responsibilities, but Tarun was old-fashioned and wanted to remain in control of everything. Even with Aarvi, he had a hard time letting go but had eventually been forced to due to health concerns.

The store employees had expressed regret that she would no longer be managing the store. It was expected, and they had known it would eventually happen. Most of them had been working at the store for many years. Their lives and livelihoods were intertwined with the past, present, and future of the bookshop. Tarun and Aarvi treated them well, paid them generously, and offered advice and resources for anything that they and their families needed.

Although Tarun was a fair and generous boss, he could at times be short-tempered. Aarvi knew that her presence had a calming influence. Her father and some employees had shared that sentiment. She managed things efficiently and kept Tarun's outbursts in check.

She also knew that the employees were worried about Tarun's health. With Aarvi getting married, if Tarun fell ill again, someone else in the family would have to manage the store. They feared that such an event might prompt the family to sell the store, which would mean uncertainty for their own jobs. They would be at the mercy of the new owners.

Tarun and Aarvi had repeatedly assured the employees that they had no intention of selling the shop.

It had been with the family for generations, and they wanted to keep it that way.

When Aarvi and Tarun arrived at the store on Monday morning, they noticed small delivery vehicles outside. The employees were unloading boxes and hauling them inside. Mondays usually brought new deliveries, which meant a lot of paperwork. Aarvi quickly got down to business with the store registers, ensuring that everything that was ordered was indeed delivered.

Amid all this, Jeev came by. He spent some time chatting with Tarun while she finished her work, and then they retreated to the back of the store, where there were desks and chairs to have some tea. Unlike Aarvi, Jeev didn't come from a business family. He was the youngest son of one of the leading lawyers in Benares. His was a large, joint family with a big household.

Tarun and Jeev's father were childhood friends. Their family ties went back a few generations with marriages between distant cousins, and they had common relatives on both sides. When Jeev's parents had asked Tarun and Ritika to approve their union, it hadn't come as a surprise to either of them. Aarvi and Jeev had known each other since childhood. They had grown up together and gone to the same school and college. It was understood that at some point they would get married.

Jeev had been a good student and had landed himself a cushy job in one of the city's large, public-sector enterprises. Aarvi and Jeev were fond of each other and looking forward to their wedding. Although their families had arranged it, they had always talked about spending their lives together.

Once in a while, Jeev would stop by the bookshop to meet Aarvi, and she quite liked his visits to take her mind off the daily routine. Their friends, well-wishers, and relatives were quite aware of their family history and upcoming wedding. As a result, they were used to seeing them together at different venues around town. Had that not been the case, the time they spent together would have been viewed with some consternation in a conservative town like Benares.

"Busy day?" Jeev asked, gesturing to a stack of books behind them that still needed to be shelved.

"Yes," Aarvi sighed. "Mondays usually are with all the new stuff coming in."

"Well, I guess you don't have to worry about it for too long. Once we are married and settled in, all this will be behind you."

Aarvi had grown up accepting the norm that after her wedding, she was expected to move into her groom's household and manage the day-to-day affairs there. Her parents had programmed her into believing that once she was Jeev's wife, her primary responsibility would be to take care of her household. And if that meant foregoing a job or career, so be it. She hadn't objected to any of that. The only thing that concerned her was that she would be moving into a large, joint family. She would have to adjust not only to Jeev, but to the extended family as well.

She had spoken to Jeev about having their own home, and he was pursuing that with his employer. The public-sector company did provide accommodations for its employees, although preference was given to folks from out of town. Jeev had made a request but hadn't yet told his family about it. He figured he would do so once he managed to get an apartment. Aarvi, for her part, hadn't pressed the issue any further. However, now that they were getting married, she was anxious about whether they could get their own place.

"Any news on the request for housing?"

"Not yet," Jeev responded.

"Do you think it will come, though?"

"Eventually, yes. Don't worry about it. We can always rent a place if we want."

"Yes, but your family wouldn't be happy." Aarvi sighed again.

"We will cross that bridge when we get to it," Jeev said affectionately.

Aarvi turned to her fiancé. "Hey, Jeev, do you know Hari Das?"

"Of course," he said with a mischievous smile, taking another sip from his teacup.

"What's with the smile?"

"He is known to be a crazy fellow, into conspiracy theories. He writes to elected officials, newspapers, the police, basically anyone who will listen to him."

"About what?" she asked.

"What they should be doing and how they can do their jobs better. He is one of those who feels that everyone's doing a shoddy job. Anyway, I heard about him at work too. My colleagues who dealt with him found him to be quite nosy."

"How so?"

"Well, he worked at the state electricity board. Our company deals with the board regularly, being a supplier. My bosses said he used to come up with theories on how folks are stealing electricity, fudging meters, et cetera."

"What's wrong with that? Some of it is true. I have read quite a few articles in the papers about people trying to steal electricity and fudging meters," contended Aarvi.

"Right, but most of his claims were totally outlandish. He never backed them up with evidence. He even claimed that a minister had once diverted electricity for his son's wedding, which had led to power cuts in town."

Aarvi lifted her shoulders. "It could be true."

"Well, he got into trouble for that. The department launched an investigation following a complaint from one of the minister's entourage, and Hari's assertions turned out to be false. Then there was the time he accused a school principal of abusing kids."

"And?" Aarvi prodded.

"All I know is that the school wasn't happy, and neither were the parents. He also thinks our education system is completely wrong, that we are churning out worker bees and stifling any sort of innovation or creativity."

"There is some merit in that opinion," Aarvi agreed.

"Maybe, but it's hard to take him seriously when all he does is complain and harp on his crazy theories. Anyway, why the sudden interest in Hari Das?"

Aarvi fiddled with her teacup. "He called my father last week to say that Devesh Uncle had left some papers and books for me."

"You mean the professor who passed away?"

Aarvi nodded.

"What did he leave for you?" Jeev asked, taking another sip.

"I don't know."

"Did you call the professor's family? I mean, you know them, right?" Jeev continued.

"I do, and no, I haven't called them."

Jeev crossed his arms over his chest, his eyebrows knitted in thought. "How did Devesh know Hari?"

"They were friends in college. That's how my father knew them, too."

"Now that you mention it, I do recall your father talking about Devesh and Hari, and how close they were in college."

"Yes, they were good friends," Aarvi stated.

"Hmm. I am sure the professor just left you a stack of crosswords with some books," Jeev claimed.

"That's what I'm thinking," Aarvi concluded. She glanced toward the far side of the bookshop and spotted the accountant walking in. Evidently sensing that Aarvi had to attend to business, Jeev got up.

"I will leave you to it, then," he said with a smile. "Let me know how it goes with Hari and Devesh's parting gift."

"Sure," Aarvi replied and gave Jeev a hug before he left the store. She walked back to her desk, picked up the stack of papers that she had carefully arranged in a file, and sat down with the accountant.

After lunch, Aarvi surveyed the store. Satisfied that everything was in order, she walked out and started toward Hari's house. Outside, the ghat was brimming with tourists, some taking pictures and others standing in line to embark on boat rides. The Ganges gleamed in the afternoon sun, and a gentle breeze provided some much needed relief from the piercing heat. The narrow streets of the city were still busy. As she moved farther away from the store and Assi Ghat, the sound of traffic died away.

A few tourists stopped her to ask for directions. Aarvi often wondered about the young backpackers who came from abroad and spent months in the city, enjoying every aspect of it. She often engaged in lengthy conversations with them about where they came from and what they liked and disliked about Benares. What surprised her was the ease with which these young foreigners took time off from work or university to ship off to a strange land without an agenda. Aarvi's life had always been structured, and she liked it that way. She could never comprehend just leaving everything behind and embarking on a journey without a plan or destination in mind. She did appreciate their sense of adventure, and she often wondered whether Indians, in general, were built differently from these foreign backpackers.

She turned onto a road lined with bungalows and glanced at a scrap of paper on which she had written Hari's address. This road was unlike the other streets that Aarvi had just walked past, which featured apartment buildings and townhomes. Small individual houses with a front porch and courtyard bespoke a picturesque life, and some had a tiny garden. She stopped in front of an old bungalow that had been freshly painted, a small garden situated past the rickety gate. She strolled through the gate and knocked on the main door. An older gentleman with thick glasses opened it.

"Hello, Aarvi."

"Hello, Uncle."

"Glad you are here as well," the gentleman said with a smile as he stepped aside, opening the door wide for Aarvi to enter.

She entered a small, sparsely furnished drawing room with a sofa and some armchairs around a coffee table. On the far side, near a window, was a small dining table with four chairs. On one wall was a large bookcase bursting with books and photographs, and the other wall held some paintings and a big photograph of what looked like the Himalayas. A young man was sitting on the sofa.

"Is this a good time, or should I come back later?" Aarvi asked.

"No, it's good that you came now. This is Mahesh Pal. He is here from Delhi for the same reason you are," Hari said.

The young man got up, and Aarvi realized he was much taller than she had first thought. They shook hands, and Aarvi sat down on an armchair across from the sofa with Hari settling into the chair beside her. Aarvi could see that he was restless, and Mahesh seemed to notice that as well. He fixed his eyes on Hari before speaking up. "Is something wrong, sir? Are you looking for something?"

"Oh no. It's just that it would be easier to talk if both of you were sitting across from me. Aarvi, do you mind sitting on the sofa next to Mahesh?"

"Not at all," Aarvi replied, complying with the strange request.

Mahesh moved aside slightly to give her more space. The sofa was large enough to seat three people. It was just that the request seemed strange. Once Aarvi had settled in, a housekeeper brought them some lemonade, placing it on the coffee table.

"Please, help yourself," Hari said, pointing to the glasses.

"Thank you," Mahesh and Aarvi said in unison.

"Now, I am glad that both of you are here at the same time. This saves me the trouble of repeating myself. Do you know why you were summoned here?" Hari asked.

"Something that Devesh Uncle left for me, and I am guessing for Mahesh too," Aarvi replied, glancing quickly toward Mahesh. He concurred with a slight nod.

"That's right," Hari replied. "Devesh left me a letter stating that he had left something for a few of his students. Mostly, they were books that he was quite fond of. For the two of you, he left some books as well as crosswords. It seems, at least from the letter, that both of you are into solving crossword puzzles. Is that true?"

"Yes," Aarvi replied, followed by a nod from Mahesh.

"Good. Here's what you have to do. Go to Devesh's home; find that useless nephew of his, Laxman, and his wife, Rani; and retrieve what Devesh has left for you. I know you are a local, Aarvi, but Mahesh, you have to head back to Delhi. How long are you here?" Hari asked, his eyes boring into Mahesh.

"I am taking the train back to Delhi early on Sunday morning."

"Why the rush?" Hari tilted his head to the side.

"I have to see my parents. And then next weekend, I leave for London."

"Ah, quitting India, I see." Hari continued with a wry smile, "might as well. This country is going to the dogs. The politicians have made a mess of it, and the people here are electing clowns and jackasses. Our education system is based on mugging and vomiting—a test of memory more than anything else. It's a good thing you are bolting."

Judging from his wide-eyed expression, Aarvi sensed that Mahesh had no idea how to react to those comments. He kept quiet as Hari turned his gaze toward Aarvi. She was annoyed with Hari's depiction of India, although she did somewhat agree with his portrayal of the politicians. Before Hari could say anything more, Aarvi decided to make things clear.

"I am not leaving. I am staying right here," she said with a finality in her voice that made Mahesh smile.

"That's good to know," Hari said. "You are getting married, right? Tarun told me, and I did get an invitation."

"That's right," Aarvi replied. It was not uncommon in large Indian weddings for parents to invite their friends without the knowledge or consent of their daughter.

"Another institution going down the drain," Hari declared.

Both Aarvi and Mahesh sighed. Before she could react, Mahesh stepped in. "I take it you are not married, sir?"

"Oh, I was. You see, my views on this unholy union are that of an insider. It is because I have been married that I have this informed and objective opinion."

Aarvi realized that it was pointless continuing this line of conversation with the old man. He could drone on forever about everything that was wrong with the country and his marriage. She could sense that Mahesh felt the same way and was glad when he brought the conversation back on track.

"If you don't mind my asking, sir, how did you get your letter?"

"It seems Devesh had left letters and notes for his friends and relatives," Hari responded.

"Oh," Mahesh said, glancing at the coffee table and, after a brief pause, continued. "Did he know he was dying?"

"No. I think he had prepared himself for the eventuality. When he passed away, his nephew called me to let me know that he had found letters and notes addressed to various people. The only reason Laxman told me is because Devesh had mentioned the subject during his limited outings following his accident. He also said that he would be donating and giving away his books and other belongings to his friends and students. It would look awkward for Laxman and Rani if they didn't follow through with the request. Mind you, none of the letters were in sealed envelopes. Those two certainly read whatever Devesh wrote."

Before Aarvi could ask further questions, the phone in the next room rang. Hari immediately got up.

"I have to take this call. It's from my bank. Another wretched institution. I tell you, if there was a better place to keep my money, I would," Hari grumbled. He parted the curtains on the door and stepped inside the adjoining room.

Aarvi could hear Hari talking on the phone and realized the conversation might take a while. That gave her and Mahesh a chance to talk to each other.

"How did you know the professor?" Mahesh asked Aarvi in a low voice.

"A friend of my father's. When he moved back to Benares, he started coming to our bookshop. He used to help us put together the crossword each month for a newsletter that we put out."

"Ah yes. He loved those."

"How about you? Was he your prof in Delhi?" Aarvi inquired.

"Not quite. He taught biology in the science department, and I studied history. We connected through the college magazine. He was the faculty member in charge of the publication. The only content he put together was the crossword."

"I am not surprised," Aarvi said with a smile. "I quite liked him, you know. Were you close to him?"

"See, that's the thing. I didn't particularly think that I was. I saw him maybe once or twice a month. The only thing we shared was our love for crosswords and Scrabble. That's why I am surprised that he left something for me. I'd have thought that he was closer to his own students or members of his faculty."

"Did you keep in touch with him after he came back to Benares?" Aarvi continued.

"Sadly, I didn't. I told him that I was pursuing a master's at JNU before he left, and that was it."

"Then it was Hari Uncle who contacted you."

"Yes. Trust me, I'd have remembered if I had met him before. I am sorry, but I have to ask. Is he like this with everyone, or are we just getting some sort of strange treatment?" Mahesh asked, and Aarvi couldn't help but smile.

"No. He is like this with everyone. It's hard to take him seriously. I do want to collect what the professor left me, though. Don't you?"

"Yes, I had called Laxman and Rani from Delhi, saying I'd pick up the box this evening. Do you want to come with me? You can pick up your stuff too. I have a car, and I can drop you back," Mahesh said, glancing toward the curtain to the adjoining room. Hari was still on the phone.

Mahesh's request took Aarvi by surprise. Normally, she wouldn't accept such an offer from a stranger. In fact, she would generally have been offended. However, Mahesh, like Aarvi, seemed confused by what Devesh had bequeathed to them, and his offer was genuine. There was also something about Mahesh that was different, and she couldn't put a finger on it. She found herself going against what she would have otherwise done and accepted his offer.

"I can give you the address of my bookstore, and you can pick me up there," she said.

"Sure," Mahesh replied.

"By the way, I do agree with you. He is a strange man," Aarvi whispered, pointing to the room where Hari was talking on the phone.

Mahesh chuckled. "It's a good thing you are here. I arrived half an hour before you did, and I was listening to him all by myself. Now I don't feel so cornered."

"Scared you, did he?" Aarvi asked with a smirk.

"Somewhat. I don't know him, and I certainly don't want to judge him based on this short conversation. First impression, though—it's hard not to think that he is not all there."

"Yes," said Aarvi with a sigh, "you do have a point."

Before they could continue, Hari came back and settled into the chair across from Aarvi and Mahesh.

"I stand corrected. Banks are not wretched institutions. They are government-appointed robbers. That's what they are. Well, enough of them and that. Where were we?"

"The things that Professor Tripathi left us," Mahesh said quickly, not wanting the subject to change to anything else. They had both had enough of Hari's theories and opinions.

"Ah yes, of course!" Hari bellowed. "So, when are you picking up the papers?"

"This evening," Aarvi replied.

"Good," Hari said, satisfied with the answer.

"If you don't mind my asking, sir, how did Professor Tripathi die?" Mahesh asked.

Hari's expression suddenly grew serious. For a minute or so, silence hung in the air. He clenched his fists and shook his head. "You see, I had written to the papers and the police commissioner about it, but no one takes me seriously."

I wonder why that is, Aarvi thought.

"About what, sir?" Mahesh asked.

A Poet's Ballad, A Crossword Mystery

Of all the things that they had heard from Hari Das this afternoon, it was what he said in response to this that startled Aarvi the most. "Officially, he died of a heart attack. That's what his nephew said. But I know there was nothing wrong with his heart. I think he was killed—murdered—and no one wants to find out why."

Professor

Aarvi had asked Mahesh to pick her up at the bookstore around 6:00 p.m. That would give her enough time to finish her work at the shop. The strange conversation with Hari Das had left her both curious and apprehensive. She was well aware of his reputation, and she knew that his theories were mostly just that. However, a part of her wanted to know whether there was any truth to what Hari believed had happened to Devesh Tripathi. She had briefly chatted with Mahesh after they had left Hari's residence, and she could sense that Mahesh was thinking about the same thing.

* * *

Mahesh made his way back to the guesthouse after the encounter with Hari Das. He was glad that Aarvi had been there, not only for the discussion with Hari, but also for the planned visit to the late professor's residence. He felt more comfortable that he wasn't in this mysterious affair alone. When she had told him of her interest in crosswords and Scrabble, Mahesh had liked her right away.

He had arrived in Benares just that morning, and although the overnight train journey had been relaxing, he was tired. Karan had picked him up at the station and driven him to the guesthouse. They had chatted briefly until Karan had to leave. It was a busy time for his family business, and Karan had promised that he would come by in the evening to give Mahesh a tour of the city. He had left Mahesh with a car and a driver that he could use during his stay in Benares. That was a godsend, as Mahesh wouldn't have to rely on public transport to get around town.

The guesthouse was the same one he had stayed in when he had visited for Karan's wedding. It was next to the Ramnagar Fort. A few tourists were staying there, mostly backpackers. The two-story guesthouse straddled the banks of the Ganges with Mahesh's room on the upper floor overlooking the river. He couldn't have hoped for better accommodations in terms of location and convenience.

The ground floor had two large halls with dorms that contained bunk beds for students. The upper floor had ten private rooms that were spacious by Benares standards. These were earmarked for families and folks coming for long-term stays. Mahesh's room was small, but more than enough for his needs. It had a single bed, a small sofa, a desk, and a chair. The ceiling fan was oversize for the room, and the walk-in closet and attached bathroom were perfect for a single person staying for a few days. One large window overlooked the river, and there was a small air conditioner that was functional but noisy.

Luckily, Mahesh didn't need the AC. Opening the large window and putting the fan on was sufficient. From the window, he could see tourists and pilgrims near the banks of the river. Some tourists were snapping pictures on the steps leading up to the embankment. He had brought his camera and decided to take some photos during his visit. As he looked sideways facing north, he saw one side of the Ramnagar Fort. It was not as famous as the ghats and the temples, but it was worth a visit for its scenic location overlooking the Ganges.

A Poet's Ballad, A Crossword Mystery

The fort had been built in the eighteenth century and belonged to the Maharaja of Benares, although the titles of the royal families had been abolished more than a decade ago. The family had opened a large portion of the fort to the public. Apart from the residence, the fort also had a museum and a temple. What it was best known for, besides being constructed from sandstone, were its courtyards, towers, balconies, and a beautiful archway.

From his research, Mahesh knew the museum housed costumes, jewelry, swords, and a vast array of vintage American cars. There was also a large astronomical clock that had seen better days. The clock had been made in the mid-nineteenth century by a famous astronomer. During its prime, it could not only tell the time but also provide details about the location of the sun, moon, and other planets.

At around 5:30 p.m., Mahesh was in the back seat of his car, an Ambassador, crossing the Ganges to pick up Aarvi. The guesthouse and Assi Ghat were on opposite sides of the river. As the car crept across Shastri Bridge, Mahesh got a full glimpse of the Ganges down the center. At this hour, he could see several boats taking tourists up and down the river. The banks were filling up with tourists and pilgrims in preparation for the evening Arti, during which hundreds of small earthen lamps would be lit and released onto the river. At night, the glittering lights floating in the water were a feast for the eyes. It was still early for all of that.

Mahesh struck up a conversation with the driver, Sukhdev. He was from Benares and gave Mahesh a rundown of the latest news and political gossip in the city and state. This was a different India than the one Mahesh knew in Delhi. Once they had crossed the bridge, the traffic slowed to a crawl. Mahesh kept glancing at his watch, figuring that he would be a few minutes late. Sukhdev parked the car a few blocks from Assi Ghat and requested that Mahesh walk the rest of the way to the bookstore and bring Aarvi back to the car.

It was a good suggestion, Mahesh realized as he started walking. A big procession of pilgrims crowded the two lanes leading to the ghat. Cars on the street had come to a standstill. Fortunately, finding the bookstore wasn't difficult. Everyone knew it by name. Once he reached the front of the shop, he was impressed by its size and overall look. The large store stood out from the other ones in the area. Although it was housed in an old building, the inside looked modern, clean, and spacious.

He stepped into the crowded shop and headed toward the cash counters. He asked an employee for Aarvi and was asked to take a seat behind a desk close to the entrance. He politely told the employee that he would browse the books on the floor while waiting. When the clerk disappeared to find Aarvi, Mahesh wandered toward the nearest aisle. As he made his way down the row of bookcases, brushing past some customers, he reached a section that had a collection of books on Benares. He picked up a large one with pictures and started leafing through it, marveling at the photographs on each page.

Footsteps sounded behind him, and before he could turn around, he heard a familiar voice. "See something you like?"

Mahesh turned around to see a smiling Aarvi, who looked different in her work attire.

"This is an impressive store. I love bookshops, and I have been to a few in various cities. I must say, this is one of the best I've visited."

"I'm glad you like it," Aarvi said.

"I love the layout as well—lots of spaces for people to move around, browse, sit. I haven't had time to see the collection, but judging from the sheer volume of books I see, it must be quite extensive."

"I will give you a tour if you come by in the afternoon during the week. Usually, afternoons are quiet, and I can show you our collection upstairs. Since you are a historian, you might like what you see."

"Historian?" Mahesh grinned. "Not quite there yet, but I will take you up on your offer. How about tomorrow afternoon? Will that work for you?"

"Sure," Aarvi replied.

"Should we get going now?"

"Yes, we should. It will take us a while to get to Devesh Uncle's house. It's quite far from here. Can you please give me a minute? I need to tell my father, and then we will be on our way."

"Absolutely," Mahesh said as he returned the book neatly on the bookshelf.

"Come. You can meet the owner of the store," Aarvi said with a smile.

Mahesh followed her toward the exit. Just before the main door, she turned toward the large desk beside the cashiers. An older gentleman sat there talking to some customers and showing them maps. Aarvi strolled up to him and whispered something in his ear. He excused himself and walked over to where Mahesh was standing.

"Hi, Mahesh. I am Aarvi's father, Tarun."

"Good afternoon, sir," Mahesh said as he gently bowed.

Tarun looked a lot like Aarvi and had a pleasant disposition. He greeted Mahesh warmly and gently placed his hand on his shoulder. "So, you are the other one that Devesh left something for."

"So it would seem, sir," Mahesh said.

"Right. Aarvi tells me you have come from Delhi and that you like the store."

"Love it, sir. Very impressive," Mahesh said with a smile, and that seemed to please Tarun.

"That's good. Well, you must come by before you go back to Delhi."

"I will, sir."

The man paused, peering at Mahesh through squinted eyes. "You remind me of someone I used to know during my college days."

"Oh?" Mahesh smiled.

"From Delhi, you say," Tarun said thoughtfully.

"Yes, sir."

"Good. Well, I won't keep you, then." Tarun grinned and turned toward his desk. He quickly nodded at Aarvi and returned to his work.

"Bye," Aarvi called before walking with Mahesh toward the exit.

* * *

Tarun continued staring at the door, puzzled. It was rather uncharacteristic of his daughter to go somewhere with someone she had just met. The only boy she had gone out with on her own, apart from her relatives, was her fiancé. She rarely entertained advances from other boys, much less from strangers. *She must like him*, Tarun thought.

He didn't think much of it. He knew that Aarvi was a responsible girl. He wondered what his wife would think if she knew that Aarvi was heading off somewhere with a boy from Delhi, even if it was only for a few hours. He shuddered at the thought, deciding not to tell her. Mahesh would be going back to Delhi, and Aarvi would marry Jeev. There was no reason for Ritika to know anything about Mahesh.

* * *

After leaving the store, Mahesh and Aarvi started toward the car. It was difficult to have a conversation while pushing through the throng of pilgrims, many of whom were chanting and singing. Before long, they were seated in the back of the Ambassador. Aarvi was glad to finally be on their way to Devesh Tripathi's house, which was far from the ghats and the town center. She was excited to find out what Devesh had left for them. She wondered if Mahesh felt the same.

After crossing a few crowded intersections, the car picked up speed. Sukhdev told Aarvi and Mahesh that it would take half an hour to reach the address. After looking out the window for a few minutes, Aarvi turned to Mahesh. "First time in Benares?"

"No, I have been here a couple of times. My mother went to Benares Hindu University," Mahesh stated, peering out the window and then turning to look at her.

"Oh, so she is from here?"

"She is actually from Calcutta, but came here for her degree."

"When was your last visit?" Aarvi continued. She could see that Mahesh was lost in thought. She wondered if he was nervous about finding out what Devesh had left for them.

"A few months ago, for a friend's wedding. This is actually his car and driver."

"Really? Where does he live?"

"On the other side of the river. His family owns a few guesthouses, and I am staying in one of them. The Old Fort Lodgings near the Ramnagar Fort."

"Ah yes. I have been there to drop off our monthly newsletter a few times."

After a while, Mahesh turned to Aarvi with a curious expression. "Why do you think the professor left stuff for us?"

"I have been wondering about that. I probably knew him a bit better than you did. Benares may seem crowded, but it really is rather small when it comes to social circles. I have spoken a few times to Rani at functions and events. I can't say we are close, but we do have common friends. One of my cousins went to school with her."

"You mentioned that your father, Hari Das, and Devesh Tripathi were classmates in college," Mahesh said.

"They were in different programs but same batch. They were good friends. Of course, after Devesh Uncle left for Delhi, they weren't in touch apart from the occasional phone call and greeting card. When he came back to Benares after his retirement, Hari Uncle visited the store regularly up until his accident, mainly to put together the monthly crossword puzzle. To be honest, I spoke to him much more during those visits than my father did."

"It's probably because you like crosswords as much as he did," Mahesh declared.

"Yes, and you mentioned that you do as well."

Mahesh nodded. "That's the only common thread I can find between us and Devesh."

"He did leave books for some of his other students, too. At least, that's what Hari Uncle said."

"All this is a bit strange, don't you think? Even Hari Das is a bit weird," Mahesh remarked.

"Are you implying that everyone in Benares is strange?" Aarvi asked with a mischievous smile.

"Maybe. I don't know. But I will keep an open mind. Two is a small sample size, but three out of three will make me think otherwise, even in a city this big."

Aarvi raised an eyebrow. "I am guessing I am the third?"

"Yes. The jury is still out. I don't know you well enough to decide just yet."

Aarvi laughed, turning to look outside. They had stopped at an intersection, and the streetlights were slowly blinking on. A gentle breeze flowed through the open windows. Soon the big Ambassador turned onto a highway.

"You said in Hari's house that you are getting married?" Mahesh asked.

"Yes," Aarvi replied, looking at him. "Next weekend."

"Congratulations."

"Thank you. How about you?"

"I am not getting married," Mahesh declared.

Aarvi chuckled. "That's not what I meant. You are going abroad for higher studies. Where are you headed?"

"University College London. I finished my master's at JNU, and now I will be joining UCL as a PhD student."

"Is that what you want?"

"Yes," Mahesh replied, looking a little taken aback by that question.

"You don't want to get married and settle down?" Aarvi asked.

"I wanted to study more," Mahesh maintained.

"And your parents are fine with that?" Aarvi asked hurriedly, surprised by his answer.

"Not quite. They would have preferred if I went back to Calcutta, joined the family business, and married someone."

Aarvi nodded. "Makes sense."

"To them, yes. But I don't want to be part of the family business."

"Why not? Wouldn't it be easier all around?"

"Easier, yes. I am not interested in it, though," Mahesh said, glancing away.

"So, you sort of went against your family's wishes."

"Yes. I mean, we *did* discuss it," Mahesh replied, averting his gaze sideways, then toward the front.

"Hmm. Are they upset with you?" Aarvi asked.

"I think they are slowly coming around."

"It must be hard for them, loving you so much, and now you are not listening to what they want," Aarvi remarked.

There was a slight pause before Mahesh responded. She could sense he was pondering before he continued. "Love and obedience are two different things. Just because someone's obedient doesn't mean they love you, and just because someone's rebellious doesn't mean that they are not affectionate."

Aarvi stared at her hands in her lap. She hadn't been brought up like that. She felt there was some truth to Mahesh's words, but she had always done what her parents had told her, abided by what they had decided for her. The only time she had insisted on something was when she had wanted to complete her degree before marrying. That hadn't been difficult since she had had allies in her father and her fiancé. Her mother had only agreed once the rest of the family had. Pushing the thoughts from her mind, she turned to Mahesh and changed the subject.

"Is UCL a good university for your PhD?"

"I believe so, at least from the research that I have done."

"Unfortunately, as you can imagine, most of us have only heard of Oxford or Cambridge. I'm sure there are many other good universities in England, but we are not aware of those," Aarvi claimed.

"That's true. Those two are the best and the most well known. I tried getting into them, but I couldn't. My grades were not good enough. But I am happy I got into UCL. I like my supervisor, and although I am a bit nervous, I am looking forward to it."

His candid admission surprised Aarvi. Usually, her friends and acquaintances would brag about where they had been admitted and the university they attended. They would never readily admit that they weren't good enough to get into a better school.

"I am sure you will do fine."

"I hope so. How about you? Have you always been in Benares?"

"Yes, my family has been here for generations. I went to school here and then to Benares Hindu University for my bachelor's."

"Wow, BHU is a good university. You must have been a good student."

"I was," Aarvi said, averting her eyes. She was happy that Mahesh was impressed with her academic ability. How much did that matter now that she was getting married and would be a homemaker in a large, joint family? Somehow, talking to Mahesh was making her think of these things. She had wondered about them sometimes, but never as much as she was now.

"We had a few students from BHU in JNU doing their master's. They were all good students."

"Were they strange?" Aarvi asked with a sly smile.

"Somewhat, but you know I can tolerate that," Mahesh said with a laugh.

Sukhdev announced they would arrive in a few minutes. They entered a sparsely populated residential neighborhood on the outskirts of the city. The small houses lining the street boasted expansive gardens and courtyards in front. A few people were enjoying their evening walks, and some children were playing in a park farther afield.

The Ambassador rolled to a stop in front of a modest, two-story house with a small front garden beyond a metal gate. Aarvi opened the gate, which gave a long screech, with Mahesh following her inside. They stepped onto the pathway leading up to the main door. After a gentle knock, the door was opened by someone who looked like the help. He led them into a drawing room and study.

Mahesh and Aarvi sat side by side on a sofa across from a large desk. As they waited, they surveyed the room. From the marks on the floor, it seemed like the furniture had been moved around a lot. After a few minutes, a gentleman who must have been in his late thirties or early forties walked in with a newspaper. He looked at Mahesh and nodded. Then he looked at Aarvi. "Hello, Aarvi. How are you?"

"I am fine, thank you. This is Mahesh. He is here from Delhi," she replied, glancing at her companion.

Mahesh got up and stretched out his hand. After a firm handshake, the gentleman asked Mahesh to sit back down. He pulled up a chair from behind the desk and sat down in front of them.

"I am Devesh's nephew, Laxman. You spoke to me and my wife, Rani, when you called from Delhi," he said, addressing Mahesh.

"Yes, sir, I remember," Mahesh replied.

"Oh, no need to call me sir. Laxman is just fine." He turned his attention to Aarvi. "Your wedding is coming up soon. Are you all set? I am sure there's a lot of preparation."

"There is. I am trying to get all of that done."

"That's good," Laxman replied. "At least you will be done with the bookstore and can start a new life."

"Yes," Aarvi murmured, not sharing Laxman's enthusiasm.

"Well, let's get to it, then. You are here for what my uncle left for you."

Aarvi and Mahesh both nodded.

"It's really a pity that you had to come all this way. I could have sent it to you in Delhi, Mahesh. As for you, Aarvi, you could have sent one of the employees from the bookshop to pick it up."

"Oh, that's all right. I don't mind," Mahesh said.

"I recall that you mentioned you were visiting a friend. At least you didn't come all the way from Delhi for this, right?" Laxman asked in a more serious tone.

Aarvi glanced at Mahesh, who paused as if to choose his words carefully before replying. "That's right. I am leaving in a couple of weeks for higher studies abroad. This gave me a chance to see my friend before I go."

"That's nice," Laxman said, slowly getting up. "If you wait here for a few minutes, I will go upstairs and get the boxes."

As he turned around, a young lady walked in. Aarvi recognized her as Rani, who said, "there's a call for you from work. It sounds urgent."

"Oh," Laxman said, heading over to the next room.

"Hi, Aarvi," Rani said with a smile before turning to Mahesh. "You must be Mahesh. I am Rani. I spoke to you on the phone."

"I remember. Nice to meet you."

"I will get the things for you," Rani said, veering toward the hallway.

"We don't mind taking it ourselves," Mahesh offered. "I know it may be in a box or something. If you can show us, we can pick it up from the professor's room."

"Oh. Our servant is still new and won't know what to do," Rani said.

"Maybe you can show us, Rani," Aarvi said with a smile.

Rani seemed to hesitate before responding, "Sure."

She led them out of the room into a corridor. Aarvi could hear Laxman having an animated conversation over the phone in a room across the hall. They continued to the staircase at the end of the corridor. Rani went up first, followed by Aarvi and Mahesh. Once they reached the upper floor, Aarvi noted that there were two doors and another, more compact door that looked like it led to a bathroom.

Rani led them to one of the rooms and turned on the lights. The large room was in a state of disarray, and it didn't seem like anyone had bothered to clean or organize it. There was only one window, the curtains were drawn, and that made it dark and damp. On the other side, a bed rested against the wall. Crutches and walking sticks were propped against the wall, probably belonging to the professor. Beside the bed was a small desk piled with papers and files. The rest of the room had shelves of various sizes jammed with books and files, some of which were scattered on the floor. There were also handwritten notes, crosswords, newspaper articles, magazines, and other documents.

While Aarvi and Mahesh waited near the door, Rani walked toward the desk, trying not to step on any of the papers. She picked up a folder and a small box from the desk, then returned to where Aarvi and Mahesh were standing. She handed the box to Mahesh and the folder to Aarvi. Their names were written on them.

Rani was about to switch off the lights and leave the room when Mahesh spoke. "Did the professor stay in this room?"

"Yes, he was here after the accident. Our room is on the same floor. It was much easier to take care of him this way rather than having to go down if he needed help."

"He was downstairs before?" Mahesh continued.

"Yes. The room that you were in was his room," Rani confirmed.

"Oh," Mahesh replied. Before he could ask anything further, Rani said, "he needed rest, and being downstairs meant that he would get disturbed every time someone came to visit or there was a phone call."

"There's no phone in this room?" Mahesh asked.

"Oh no. There's only one line, and it's in the room downstairs," Rani replied.

"If you don't mind my asking," continued Mahesh, his eyes fixed on Rani, "what happened in the accident?"

"It was sad, really," Rani said in a solemn voice. "He was coming back home after his visit to the club. When he was walking from the bus stop, a lorry hit him."

"Oh, that must have been serious?" asked Mahesh in a slightly louder tone.

"Yes, it was. He was in the hospital for a while, and when he came back, he wasn't the same. His mobility was restricted. He was mostly confined to this room, and if he did go out, we had to go with him."

"Did they catch the culprit at least?" Mahesh asked.

"No. It was probably one of those uncouth truck drivers. They are all from out of town. Real savages, the ones who drive those trucks. He didn't even stop.

There were no witnesses. Some people saw Uncle lying on the road afterward, and once they recognized him, they called us, and we took him to the hospital."

While she spoke, Rani probably didn't realize that Mahesh was also from out of town. "That must have been scary," he said. Before he could ask anything further, they heard a noise in the hallway. They turned to see that Laxman had come upstairs.

"What's going on here?" he asked, looking at his wife with a frown.

"Oh, we just came to pick up the papers," she replied defensively. Her tone seemed to suggest that she had done something wrong.

"You didn't have to bring them all the way upstairs. You could have just brought the papers and handed them over to them," admonished Laxman, glaring at his wife. Aarvi decided to step in and smooth things over.

"It's all right, Laxman. We are the ones who asked her to bring us upstairs. You know I love books, and I wanted to take the opportunity to see Devesh Uncle's collection.

It really is impressive," Aarvi said, smiling at Laxman and then glancing around the room.

Laxman's demeanor changed immediately. "Yes, Uncle loved his books and his crosswords. Books I can understand. His love for crosswords, I never did. I went through his stuff after he passed, and you can't imagine how many of these crosswords I found. You can see for yourself as you go through your things. It's some books and mostly puzzles, really useless stuff."

"I take it you are not into crosswords?" Mahesh asked politely.

"Not at all," Laxman replied. He started tapping his left foot on the floor. He turned his body slightly, gesturing that he wished to leave the room and wanted the others to follow suit.

Mahesh wanted to continue asking Laxman and Rani about the professor and the accident. Aarvi sensed it, and before Mahesh could say anything, she quickly touched his arm, gave him a pointed look, and shook her head. Then she turned to Laxman. "Is there anything else that Devesh Uncle left for us?"

"He didn't. I know it's a bit disappointing. That's why I said that I could have just sent it over to you."

"That's all right," Aarvi said with a smile.

"Well, if you have what you need, then we can head back downstairs. I am sorry to have to do this, but I need to catch up on some work. It's a busy time for me," Laxman said, hinting for them to leave.

"Sure," Mahesh replied. "Thank you so very much for having us over and giving us what the professor left for us."

Laxman grinned and opened the door wide to let them out of the room and switched off the lights. They all headed downstairs, with Rani leading the way. At the main entrance, Rani opened the door, and they all stepped outside. While Mahesh and Laxman headed toward the gate, Rani pulled Aarvi aside.

"You must be so excited about your wedding," she said, now totally relaxed.

"Yes, I am," Aarvi responded.

"Are you all set?"

"More or less."

They looked toward Mahesh and Laxman, who were now outside the gate and out of earshot. Rani then leaned closer to Aarvi.

"You know, it doesn't look good that you are going around town with another man just before getting married. I know Mahesh is from Delhi and will be returning soon. But you know how Delhi boys are. They don't have the same values or upbringing that we do. What will people think if they saw the two of you this late in the evening together?" Rani murmured in a serious tone.

"To be honest, I am not sure," Aarvi responded, not wanting to continue this conversation any further.

"Do your parents know?" Rani went on.

"Yes," Aarvi replied hurriedly. She chose not to mention that her mother was not aware of this visit, but her father had approved. Aarvi hoped that her tone conveyed how annoyed she was getting with this discussion.

"All I am saying is that Benares isn't Delhi, and people talk," Rani pressed further. The way she said it, it was clear that she knew that the conversation was making Aarvi uncomfortable. Aarvi decided to put a stop to it.

"Yes, I am well aware of that. It's a small town with lots of small people who have nothing better to do than engage in small talk," Aarvi said, which silenced Rani.

Aarvi marched toward where Mahesh and Laxman were standing by the car. After thanking Laxman, Aarvi and Mahesh were on their way back to the city.

Aarvi was still ruffled from her exchange with Rani and wondered if Mahesh had picked up on it. They gazed out the window for a few minutes before Mahesh turned to Aarvi. "What was that all about?"

"What do you mean?"

"You and Rani. I could tell from your body language that you were arguing," Mahesh commented.

"Not really. She was just giving me some unsolicited advice."

"About what?"

"You."

"Me?" Mahesh asked, his pitch rising an octave.

"She was telling me to watch out for Delhi boys. Apparently, you are up to no good and don't have the same values as good Benares boys."

"And what are those values?"

"I don't know. We didn't get to that, but I have to watch out, so beware," Aarvi said with a playful smirk.

"Right," Mahesh said, glancing away bashfully.

"What were you and Laxman talking about?"

"He didn't say much." Mahesh turned to face her again. "Each time I brought up something about the professor—his activities, his hobbies, or the accident—he changed the subject and started asking me about my future. He simply didn't want to talk about anything with regard to his uncle."

"And what do you think about the visit overall?"

"I found their behavior strange. They didn't want us there for long. They didn't offer us any tea or water. It seemed they wanted us to collect the stuff and leave."

"Yes, I felt the same way," said Aarvi, nodding thoughtfully. The car was now back on the highway, speeding toward the city center and Assi Ghat.

"There were other things that were odd too," continued Mahesh.

"Like what?"

"The professor's room was downstairs, and then, after the accident, they moved him upstairs. Don't you find that strange?"

"Well, as Rani said, perhaps it was to make sure they were nearby in case he needed anything," Aarvi noted.

"That doesn't make sense. If his mobility was restricted, then staying downstairs would have made more sense for getting in and out of the house," Mahesh reasoned.

"Maybe it was better for him to rest upstairs. Fewer visitors, less disturbance."

"Maybe," Mahesh said, not sounding convinced. Aarvi could sense there was more he wanted to say.

"What's bothering you?"

"The phone," Mahesh replied.

"What about it?"

"The telephone is downstairs next to where the professor's room was before they took him upstairs. Isn't that strange? I mean, if he got any phone calls, he wouldn't be able to come down and answer them. Nor would he be able to make any."

"That's true," Aarvi said, finally coming around to what Mahesh was thinking.

"It was almost as if Laxman and Rani wanted to control who visited the professor, who called him, and where he went after the accident."

"Yes, you may have a point, but why?"

"I don't know," Mahesh replied with a sigh, leaning into the back seat.

"You really wanted to visit the professor's room upstairs. Why?" Aarvi asked.

"It's because of something Hari Das told me when I first called him from Delhi."

"What did he say?"

"Hari said that the professor had insisted that I pick up the box from his nephew in person. That's why I wanted to take a look at his room."

Aarvi scoffed. "It was a mess."

"It certainly was," Mahesh agreed.

"Doesn't tell us much, does it?"

"Except that someone may have been searching for something. The room was in disarray, almost as if someone had turned the place upside down looking for something. I am not sure if they found it," Mahesh stated, and then looked away.

Aarvi was lost in thought, trying to make sense of their interaction with Laxman and Rani. Maybe Mahesh was right? *But what were they looking for?* She wondered.

"Yes, that could be the case," Aarvi said, nodding gently.

"Or maybe I am just overthinking all of this based on what Hari told us earlier this afternoon," Mahesh said, turning his head slightly toward her.

"That Devesh Uncle was killed?"

He nodded slowly. "I am not sure, but . . . "

"I wouldn't put much weight in what Hari Uncle says," Aarvi uttered before Mahesh could finish.

"But you do have to admit that there was a strange vibe in that house."

"Yes, with that I agree."

For the next few minutes, as the Ambassador inched through the crowded streets, Aarvi and Mahesh spoke about Benares and what they knew about the professor through their past interactions with him. Mahesh was easy to talk to. Unlike other boys she had met, he was not trying to impress her, but she was still impressed. He was candid in offering his opinions, and he wanted to hear what she had to say, even if he didn't agree with her. He also had a good sense of humor.

Aarvi told Mahesh about her college days, her favorite books, and her best-loved Bollywood movies. They were a mile from the bookshop, and the car had come to a complete halt. A massive procession of pilgrims was crossing the street after the evening puja near the banks of the Ganges, chanting and singing. The crowd seemed completely oblivious to the traffic jam they had caused.

"This is a regular occurrence in this part of town," Aarvi said, motioning to the sea of people chanting outside.

"That's all right, I don't mind. It just means I get to talk to you a bit more, and that's fine with me," Mahesh said with a smile.

"I bet you don't have these in Delhi."

"Oh, Delhi has its fair share of processions, but New Delhi is spread out, and the rallies and protests are usually confined to a small section of the city. The crowds are not always this peaceful at those events. Usually, people are angry. You wouldn't be able to sit in a car in the middle of a throng of people going by."

"I can imagine," Aarvi said.

While they waited, Mahesh studied the small cardboard box in his lap and quickly opened it to see what was inside.

An assortment of crosswords was piled in loose sheets with handwritten numbers on top. There were also two used books and some newspaper cuttings. Nothing else. Aarvi could tell that Mahesh was as confused as she was.

From the corner of her eye, Aarvi saw that the books were copies of Emily Brontë's *Wuthering*

Heights and F. Scott Fitzgerald's *The Great Gatsby*. The books were old and falling apart. Mahesh arranged the loose sheets of paper in order according to the numbers written on them. *There's something strange about these crosswords,* Aarvi thought. None of them were particularly big. Devesh had usually created more elaborate puzzles.

"Anything interesting?" Aarvi asked, pointing to what Mahesh was scrutinizing.

"Not sure," Mahesh said, handing over the books to her.

"These are classics. Your favorites?"

"Nope. I have read them, and I like them, but I can't say they are my favorites. I never spoke to the professor about books."

"It is unusual that he would leave you all this. Well, I have the same thing in my folder. A bunch of puzzles and a book on cooking."

"How peculiar."

"That's for sure," Aarvi concurred, and Mahesh nodded slightly.

The crowd finally behind them, the car started creeping forward.

"Do you still want me to come by the bookshop tomorrow afternoon?"

"Of course," Aarvi replied. "Why wouldn't I?"

"I mean, with what Rani said about Delhi boys and all. If you must know, I am originally from Calcutta. I moved to Delhi for my bachelor's and master's."

"Right, so I think just because of that, you are fine," Aarvi said, grinning.

"Thank you. I was worried for a while," Mahesh responded, sighing in mock relief.

Now that they were just a few minutes from the bookshop, Aarvi suggested that the driver take another lane that would be less crowded. Mahesh took out a pencil and started working away at the first crossword. A short time later, the car stopped in front of the bookstore. There was still half an hour before closing time.

Aarvi had told her father that she would be coming back to the store and they would go home together.

She didn't want to risk having Mahesh drop her home. If her mother saw her with another boy, Aarvi would have to endure a meaningless and painful line of questioning. Aarvi glanced sideways at Mahesh and realized that he wasn't paying attention; he was solely focused on the puzzle. She wasn't sure if he knew that the car had stopped, and he had a strange look on his face as he stared down at the crossword.

"What's going on?" Aarvi asked.

"These are short crosswords."

"Yes, I looked at them. They are short. Nothing wrong with that."

"True, except that I have already solved the first one, and the horizontal and vertical sets make two sentences," Mahesh mumbled.

"What are they?" Aarvi asked, curious as to why he looked both puzzled and lost.

"Take a look," Mahesh said, handing her the sheet.

She looked at the paper. He had solved the crossword and then written two sentences in pencil at the very bottom. What she read made her stomach drop.

His death was unnatural. The answers are all in the books.

She locked eyes with Mahesh. "So maybe Hari Uncle was right."

"Yes, and we have to solve the crosswords to get to the bottom of it."

Crosswords

After dropping Aarvi at the bookshop, Mahesh headed to the guesthouse. The receptionist at the front desk informed him that Karan had called and said he would be stopping by after dinner. Mahesh decided to freshen up and then grab something to eat at the guesthouse canteen.

After supper, he sat in the courtyard overlooking the Ganges, a gentle breeze making the evening more pleasant. A few people were strolling near the banks, and at this time of night, the crowds were sparse. He struck up a conversation with some tourists. There were backpackers from Europe, some yoga enthusiasts from the United States, and, of course, travelers and pilgrims from all over India.

After an hour, Mahesh returned to his room to start examining the box from Devesh a little more closely. He pulled out the contents and arranged them neatly in three piles on his small desk. The first pile comprised all the crossword puzzles in numerical order. The second one featured all the other paper cuttings. The last one was the two books.

He started with the books, slowly leafing through the pages. It was evident that they were well used. The covers were worn out, and the spines betrayed that they had gone through several readers. There were handwritten notes on several pages with different sets of handwriting, a few words underlined and some encircled. He had read both books and wondered why the professor would leave them in the box.

Next, he shifted his attention to the pile of newspaper cuttings and fliers. They were news items from mainly sports stories, plus a few editorials on current events. That surprised Mahesh. From the little interaction he had had with Devesh, he knew the man had not really been interested in sports. He would rarely include clues in the crosswords that had anything to do with athletics. Finally, he looked at the pile of crossword puzzles. He picked up a pencil to start solving the second one, but a knock on the door interrupted him.

It was Karan. He had arrived with a flask of hot tea, sweets, and samosas. They immediately embraced, and Karan made himself comfortable on the small sofa while Mahesh sat on the bed with his back against the wall. They reminisced about their days in college, feeling like two old friends who could talk forever. Although they hadn't kept in touch, seeing Karan reminded Mahesh of his most pleasant memories. After almost two hours of laughter, jokes, and friendly banter, they had polished off their snacks, and it was getting close to midnight. It was only then that their conversation shifted to the present.

"How is married life treating you?" Mahesh asked.

"It has its moments. I think it's more of an adjustment for women, at least in my case."

"I can imagine. It's not easy coming into a joint family. Has Suneeta settled in?"

"Not quite," said Karan with a sigh. "It's still a work in progress, and you are right. It's difficult. I know she is trying her best, but as you know, my family is a bit old school, and sometimes things get awkward."

"Have you ever thought of moving out with Suneeta and living on your own?"

"It may come to that eventually. But my parents and brothers wouldn't be happy," Karan noted.

"Do you really care?" Mahesh asked.

He could see Karan hesitating slightly before responding. "Beyond a certain point, no. But not everyone is like you."

"What does that mean?"

"Rebellious, giving up on the family business, striking out on your own."

Mahesh stared down at the bed. "It doesn't feel that way. I wish my parents would be proud of me."

"Well, to me it does. It's not easy, what you have done. I wish I could be more forceful sometimes," Karan said.

"How so?"

"I took the easier option, joined the family business. And I am not complaining. It comes with its perks. I don't have to be in the rat race like everyone else, looking for a job, trying to please my boss, worrying about my next promotion, et cetera."

"All good, then?"

"But there's another side to it. I am expected to comply with my family's wishes. We never talk about it, but it's well understood that if I don't go with what they say, they could ask me to leave," Karan professed.

Mahesh could see that Karan was struggling with this, but he could also sense that he wanted to talk about it. "They do take your opinion on things, though, right?" he asked.

"They do. But I am the youngest in the family, and my father makes all the decisions. At the end of the day, the most I get is a patient hearing, and then we all have to do what he decides."

The corner of Mahesh's mouth lifted in a half smile. "Yeah, well, my father's probably the same. I don't know, maybe subconsciously it could be one of the reasons I am going abroad. Is that dynamic causing you problems?"

"It wasn't till I got married. Now things are different. There are things that Suneeta and I want to do, and we always have to get permission and make sure it's okay with the rest of the family. That can be stressful," Karan said and sighed.

"Did something happen recently?"

"Well, sort of. We wanted to take some time off and go to Goa. But my father and brothers decided that it wasn't a good time. They said I have to take care of business during the summer months, which are usually busy. So, we had to put it off until later. This sort of thing puts a lot of strain on the marriage."

"I can't say that I understand. I hope things do get better for both of you," Mahesh said, and paused. He wasn't sure how he could help Karan, but he knew that talking about it made him feel better. He could see Karan's expression change slightly, and soon he had a smile on his face.

"Yeah, we'll see. Enough about me—let's talk about what happened today. Did you get what you came here for from the Tripathis?"

"Yes, everything that you see on the desk," Mahesh replied, pointing to the stacks of books and papers.

Karan rose from the sofa and started sifting through the contents on the desk. He picked up the two books and then looked at the other two piles of paper.

"This is all he left you?" Karan inquired, pointing to the desk.

"Before I get into that, tell me, what do you think of the professor's family?"

"He didn't have one. He lived with his nephew," Karan responded, poring over the contents on the table.

"That's what I meant. Do you know much about Laxman and Rani?" Mahesh asked, changing his posture to sit slightly more upright.

"Not really. They did come to my wedding with the professor. We see them at functions and other events, but I can't say I know them well. Why?"

"What does Laxman do? Do you know?"

"Ah yes. He is in real estate, some sort of developer. I only know this because his company purchased some land next to one of our guesthouses just outside Benares," Karan said.

"It's his company?"

"His and a few others'. I think one of his partners approached my father about investing, but he refused. What's this about? Why the sudden interest in Laxman and Rani?"

Mahesh proceeded to tell Karan about the letter he had received, his conversations with Hari Das, his visit to the Tripathi residence earlier that evening, and his discussion with Aarvi. Karan listened without interruption. When Mahesh pointed to the crossword that he had solved, Karan stared at it and Mahesh gave him some time to digest everything.

"What about Hari Das?" Mahesh asked.

"I don't know him, but I know *of* him. He has a bit of a reputation for being a troublemaker. No one takes him seriously," Karan noted.

"You think he may be right about the professor?"

"That Devesh was killed?"

"Yes." Mahesh continued.

"I don't know. I'd have said that it was probably one of his conspiracies, but then this first puzzle you solved makes me wonder if there's some truth to it. You would have to solve the rest of them to see if they amount to anything."

"I am planning to do that tonight."

Mahesh's thoughts returned to what had happened at the professor's residence. He was convinced that Laxman and Rani were hiding something.

"What about Aarvi? Is she doing the same? You said the professor left a folder for her too," Karan said.

"I don't know. I think she might. Do you know Aarvi?"

"I know who she is. We have exchanged pleasantries a few times when she came over to drop off their monthly newsletter at some of our guesthouses. Everyone knows their bookstore, and most locals know Tarun and his family. They are good people. I heard she is getting married soon."

"Yes, next weekend. She told me."

"What does she think of all this?" Karan asked, holding up the papers.

"I think she is a bit confused as well. From what I gather, she likes puzzles too, and I am guessing she will start solving the ones in her file tonight. It's hard not to be curious about this."

"True," Karan said, nodding.

"The only common link that we could find between us, and the professor, was that we all like crossword puzzles."

"Us, as in you and Aarvi?"

"Yes," Mahesh confirmed.

"You think the professor left each of you clues about his death?"

"I am not sure. I will have to solve the rest of the puzzles to see if that's the case. If indeed the professor felt that he was in danger, I'm surprised he didn't tell anyone," Mahesh stated, stroking his chin.

"Maybe he couldn't. Based on what you said, it seems Laxman and Rani went to great lengths to keep him isolated and under their watch. I can't say for sure, but it's not that far-fetched to think it might be a possibility."

"True. That's why I wanted to know about them."

"I can find out more. I know Suneeta and Rani have some mutual friends. I can ask her," Karan offered.

"I don't want you to get into any trouble because of this," Mahesh said, pointing to the crosswords.

"Too late for that now. In any case, if anything goes wrong, it will be your fault, and I am fine with that," Karan said with a grin, now sitting back on the sofa.

"This is all a big puzzle as of now," Mahesh said thoughtfully.

"I will tell you what's also a surprise," Karan said with a mischievous smile.

"What?"

"That Aarvi likes you," Karan announced playfully.

"Oh, come now."

"Nope, really. Their family is quite conservative. I know we are already in the eighties, but trust me when I say that Benares isn't Delhi. Also, I know the family and enough about Aarvi to know she wouldn't go anywhere with you if she didn't like you."

"It's not that big a deal. It's not like we went on a date or anything," Mahesh contended.

"I am just surprised, that's all. She just met you and doesn't even know you. Her family doesn't know you either."

"I wouldn't read too much into it," Mahesh said.

"Perhaps, but I know I am right when I say that she probably likes you."

"What's there not to like?" Mahesh said with a playful smirk.

"True, that we agree on," Karan replied, chuckling.

"Anyhow, I think—first impressions—she is a nice girl, smart, and in the same boat in terms of trying to figure out what's going on with all this," Mahesh said, gesturing to the desk.

"And pretty too."

"Yes, she is."

They talked a bit more about Benares, how different it was from Delhi, and again about Karan's family business. Although things were going well for Karan, Mahesh felt that his friend was not happy that his father and brothers weren't taking him seriously. After another hour or so, Karan left.

It was now well past midnight, and although he was tired, Mahesh let his curiosity get the better of him. He took out a writing pad and started working on the crosswords.

When he started solving the puzzles, Mahesh quickly realized why Devesh had left him the books. The clues pointed to pages and words in them. He carefully laid them out, and a picture started to emerge. Solving everything took a while. The clues weren't always straightforward, and only someone who had been solving puzzles for a while could decipher them.

The ones that weren't referencing the book were easier, giving him direct clues.

Ten-letter word across for God *starting with* P*: providence.*

Five-letter word down for ballads *starting with* P*: poems.*

Seven-letter word across for truthful *starting with* T*, ending with* D*: trusted.*

Eight-letter word down for ancestry *starting with* H*, ending with* E*: heritage.*

And on and on it went. The ones that took more time were the ones for which Mahesh had to refer to the books. He was impressed with the level of detail the professor had gone into to hide the clues. He was also startled by how many times the word *death* appeared in them.

When he finished, he looked down at his writing pad. He had already filled up many pages trying to cross-reference everything. Finally, he wrote the sentences down on a fresh page.

His death was unnatural.

The answers are all in the books.

Answers are in the language of the Vedas and Shakespeare.

Translations are the key.

His trusted aide was removed.

He now works in the club.

The book of poems in heritage is meant for the sea.

She lives in the city of the mad king.

Should providence take him prematurely, death can help.

Look for death near the Deer Park where the Buddha preached.

Gratitude to the lord of death and peace.

Mahesh reread them. They didn't make much sense. He was sleepy and decided to look at them again in the morning with a fresh mind to see if he had made any mistakes. It was nearly 4:00 a.m., and he was exhausted. Setting aside the clues, he switched off the light and went to sleep.

* * *

Meanwhile, on the other side of town, Aarvi was tossing and turning in bed. There had been a huge argument during dinner that night. When Aarvi and her father returned home, they found themselves amid a shouting match between Ashish and their mother. Ashish's high school test results had come in, and he had fared worse than expected. He had warned his family beforehand, so their expectations had already been low. But his marks were well below what he had prepared them for. He wouldn't be getting into a good college in Benares. If he wanted to pursue higher studies, he would most likely need to move to a different city, a prospect that Aarvi was convinced her brother wouldn't mind.

Arguments between Ashish and his parents were quite common. What had made things worse this time around was that Ashish's grades, and his future, would become a topic of conversation during Aarvi's wedding. Ashish and Aarvi were convinced their mother was more worried about what others would think of Ashish's test results than about the marks themselves or, for that matter, Ashish's future. The row had continued over dinner, with the entire family getting involved. Aarvi had tried her best to defend her brother but knew he hadn't studied hard for the exam and probably deserved most of the criticism being levied at him. Tarun had been quiet during most of the conversation, piping in mostly to agree with his wife.

Aarvi knew what was on her father's mind. He had spoken to her once about it. If Ashish didn't do well in his exams and couldn't get into a decent college, Tarun would coax him into working at the bookstore. However, Tarun also knew that Ashish was not interested. The few times he had come to the store to help, he had been bored and left early. His lack of interest in the business was a source of worry and disappointment for the rest of the family. Overall, the bitter dinner conversation had left Aarvi exhausted.

Once she had retired to her room, Aarvi had dived into the file from Devesh. Since her brother's poor results had dominated the dinner conversation, they had had no time to talk about what had happened at the Tripathi residence. Part of her was relieved. Aarvi wasn't quite sure how her mother would react to her going there with another boy and focusing on tasks other than her wedding. She could sense that her father didn't want to discuss it either. She was thankful for that.

Paging through the puzzles, she realized that they were short and referenced the book that was also tucked in the folder. The evening's heated events had left her with a headache, and although she was keen to get started on the puzzles, she decided to sleep and wake up early to solve them.

At around 4:00 a.m., she was awakened by a noise outside her second-floor window. She tiptoed to the windows and opened them. The sky was overcast, and the sound was only the wind rattling the shutters. She left them open to let the breeze waft into the room, bringing a refreshing chill.

Her room overlooked a large garden, the entrance gates to their residence, and the street beyond that. Some milk vans were already dropping off bottles, and a cyclist was delivering newspapers. As she gazed out the window, her thoughts drifted to Mahesh. She wanted to speak to him about the puzzles and was looking forward to his visit to the bookstore that afternoon. She found herself wanting to spend more time with him and not just to talk about what had happened to Devesh.

She picked up the folder and sat down on her bed, arranging all the papers in order. Taking out a writing pad and pen from one of her bedside table drawers, she started solving the puzzles one by one. Aarvi marveled at the extent to which Devesh had gone to create the clues for each word and reference to pages in the book. She prided herself on her crossword prowess, but it still took her a couple of hours to figure everything out. She began with the one-word clues.

A Poet's Ballad, A Crossword Mystery

Four-letter word across for servant *starting with* A: *aide.*

Five-letter word down for cessation *starting with* P: *peace.*

Nine-letter word across for benediction *starting with* G: *gratitude.*

Eleven-letter word down for hastily starting with P: *prematurely.*

Then she moved to the sentences for clues.

Human method of communication, eight letters starting with L*, ending with* E: *language*

Hindu sacred texts, five letters starting with V: *Vedas.*

Although some clues were head-scratchers, she was pleased when she finished everything. She neatly copied all the sentences, in order, on a fresh sheet of paper and scrutinized them. There were eleven sentences in all, and they didn't make much sense. She puzzled over the phrases for a few minutes and then suddenly felt sleepy. The morning sun was now creeping into her room, and the summer breeze teased of a sweltering day. She carefully tore out the paper from the writing pad, folded it, and put it in her purse before deciding to take a short nap.

She was awakened by the sound of her mother yelling from downstairs, asking her and her brother to come down for breakfast. She looked at the clock on her bedside table. It was nearly 8:00 a.m. After taking her time getting ready, she headed downstairs.

The scene around the dining table looked completely different from the night before. Her parents sat quietly at opposite ends of the table. Tarun was busy reading the newspaper, having already finished breakfast. Ashish was nowhere to be seen. Aarvi sat down and started eating her cereal in silence, not wanting to initiate any conversation. After a few minutes, Ritika spoke up.

"You need to help me with some sarees that we bought over the weekend. I need to decide which ones we are going to give to your in-laws' family members and others that we may want to give to guests from out of town."

"Sure." Aarvi sighed. She didn't want to get into an argument with her mother.

"When do you think you will have time? You seem too busy at the bookstore again."

"In the evening. I will try to be back early," Aarvi blurted, wondering if her mother could sense her irritation.

"I wish you would just stop with the bookstore and focus on your wedding."

"I already did. I think I've had enough of dealing with relatives and shopping for clothes and jewelry," Aarvi stated.

"Well, it's a happy occasion, and we should enjoy it."

"I don't see you enjoying it. All I see is everyone getting stressed about everything from the meals and guests to shopping and every other detail."

"You don't understand," Ritika pronounced.

"No, actually, I don't," Aarvi grumbled, seeing that her mother was itching for an argument. She was glad when her father quickly stepped in to diffuse the situation.

"Actually, I have asked Aarvi to help me with some work at the store. I won't be seeing her there as much once she is married. I am trying to make the most of it now," Tarun said.

That seemed to calm Ritika. She let out a long sigh and dropped the subject. Aarvi glanced at her father and gave him a smile to thank him. She quickly finished her breakfast, and as she got up to leave, Ritika turned to Aarvi. "You haven't worn that dress in a while. That really looks good on you. You should wear it more often. Anything special going on at the store?" she asked.

"No. You are right about this attire. I found it in my dresser and decided to put it on," Aarvi replied, quickly pivoting to walk away.

Tarun folded the paper and sipped on his tea, watching Aarvi. He knew there was nothing special going on at the store for Aarvi to dress better than she usually did. He wondered if it had anything to do with the boy from Delhi who would be visiting in the afternoon. He glanced at his wife, whose inquisitive expression told him she expected some sort of discussion. He smiled and quickly went back to his newspaper.

* * *

When Mahesh arrived at the Sanskriti Bookshop that afternoon, it was unusually busy. A group of tourists had just finished a boat tour near Assi Ghat and had decided to mill about the store. Tarun was talking to a few of them near the cash registers, while Aarvi was helping some backpackers pick out travel guides at the far end of the store. She waved at him and pointed to a sitting area in a corner.

On his way there, Mahesh stopped to quickly greet Tarun from afar. He could see everyone was busy. Picking up a book on the history of Benares, he settled into one of the comfortable chairs next to a large window. He peered out the window, spotting a group of pilgrims heading toward the riverbank. From the bright reflection on the water, Mahesh could tell the sun was still scorching. The cool interior of the store was a welcome change from the incessant heat outside.

Glancing toward Aarvi, he noticed that the flood of patrons was now slowly leaving the store. Tarun was back behind a counter, talking to one of his employees. The sitting area where Mahesh was stationed was quite far from where both Tarun and Aarvi stood. He leaned back in the chair and started reading the book he had picked up. After a few minutes, he heard footsteps. Aarvi was standing next to one of the chairs.

"Hi, Mahesh. How are you? Sorry about that. Usually, afternoons are quiet. But sometimes we do get a group, and it suddenly becomes busy."

"Oh, no apology needed. I am the one who should be thankful for this," Mahesh said, and got up.

"How was your morning?"

"I spent it with my friend Karan. I visited his family, and he gave me a quick tour of the city."

"He didn't want to come to the store?" Aarvi asked.

"No, he is busy this afternoon. He has been here before, but of course, he never had the honor of a tour from you," Mahesh said with a smile.

Aarvi laughed. "Come, let me show you the store. We will start with this floor and then head upstairs."

"I will let you be my guide."

Mahesh was fascinated by not only the history section, but the many books of all genres. They talked a lot about books, but they also carried out in-depth conversations about other academic subjects. They discussed their favorite authors, characters, and stories.

Once they finished with the ground floor, they headed toward where Tarun was seated. After exchanging pleasantries with Mahesh, Tarun gave Aarvi the keys to the locked section on the top floor and instructed an employee to get some tea and snacks for them. As Aarvi led him upstairs, Mahesh stopped midway at the landing to get a full view of the store from this vantage point.

"It's great that you get to work here every day."

"Yes," Aarvi replied with a sigh.

Mahesh caught the dejection in her tone. "Anything wrong?"

"No," Aarvi replied quickly. "Let's head upstairs, and I will show you the rest of the store."

"Sure," he said, dropping the subject.

They spoke about their favorite quotes and passages from books. Mahesh impressed Aarvi with his ability to recall dialogues and lines from his favorite stories.

The upper floor was largely empty. Once Aarvi had shown him the collection of rare books and papers, they sat down across a small floor desk for the tea and jalebis that Tarun had sent for them. Aarvi spoke to Mahesh about her days in college, her friends, and deeper topics that one would normally only discuss with close friends and family. Mahesh was open about his views as well, sharing things that he had tried but failed at, always lending an ear to dissenting opinions.

After they finished their tea, Mahesh glanced at his watch. They had spent almost an hour talking. Time had flown by, and they hadn't even started discussing Devesh. Aarvi broached the subject first. "I am guessing you solved the puzzles the professor left for you," she said.

Mahesh nodded. Reaching into his satchel, he pulled out a folder. He opened it to remove a writing pad from the sheaf of papers, placing it on the desk for Aarvi to see. He showed her all the sentences he had written down.

"It took me a while to solve them, and I went back and forth a few times. This is what I came up with." Mahesh pointed to the collection of enigmatic sentences.

"Oh my God, take a look at this." Aarvi reached into her purse and carefully unfolded a piece of paper, laying it on the desk. They were identical.

"I guess the professor figured either one of us or both would collect the material he left for us and then solve them," Mahesh said. "I am impressed. I consider myself quite an expert in solving crosswords, and it still took me some time to solve them. I am sure the professor knew that you were also quite good."

"Yes, I guess I am," Aarvi said with a shy smile. "I do admit that it took me a while, too. I think that's the common thread: he left these for us because he knew that we would be able to solve them. I am thinking he was counting on one of us to figure it all out. But why did he have to be so cryptic?"

"I think it all comes down to what we felt at the Tripathi residence yesterday. Laxman and Rani didn't let him out of their sight. It's quite clear that he wouldn't have been able to discuss anything or meet anyone without them present."

"I think you may be right," Aarvi said, her voice taking on a serious tone.

"Do you think there is any truth to the claim that his death was unnatural? After all, he says as much in the first sentence, and Hari Das suspects the same thing."

"Something is definitely not right. I am sure the professor felt his life was in danger. He created these puzzles and left them for us in the event of his untimely death," Aarvi proclaimed.

Mahesh pursed his lips in thought. "I guess Laxman and Rani didn't think much of it since they were just crosswords."

"That's right. I must say, it was ingenious of the professor to get these out. But why couldn't he have done this before his death? He could have warned someone, somehow."

Mahesh scrunched his eyebrows in thought. "I am not sure. Perhaps he tried, and no one believed him. Or maybe he didn't think that his nephew would put his life in danger. At this point, I am just guessing. I didn't know the professor that well, and I certainly don't know Laxman and Rani."

Aarvi released a long exhale. "Well, I do know them, more as acquaintances than friends. Honestly,

I can't imagine that they would have done something to harm the professor. But who knows?"

"We could try going to the police. But all we have are a bunch of clues from a crossword. The sentences don't even make much sense, at least as of now."

"Hari Uncle tried that. He wrote to the police, and it didn't go anywhere. They need hard evidence to follow up on. I agree this won't suffice," Aarvi said, pointing to the paper for emphasis.

They were both silent for a while, studying the crosswords and the sentences. Mahesh picked up the writing pad and looked at Aarvi. "I think we need to figure out what all these sentences mean. Maybe there are clues that lead to some sort of evidence," he said.

Aarvi nodded decidedly. "Right. Where do we start? Does the order mean something? Are we supposed to refer to the books again? I mean, look at the next sentence. It says the answers are all in the books."

"I think it means that the crosswords themselves point to the books. Do you remember the clues? Some of them were direct while others pointed to chapters and pages in the books, and only then could we come up with these sentences."

"That's right. So, we have figured out the first two sentences. I think I know what the next one means. The professor always liked putting clues from Shakespeare's plays in the newsletter. Sometimes the answers were direct translations in plain English. But he mentions the language of the Vedas."

Mahesh's eyes widened with realization. "Sanskrit. That's what he means. Translation between English and Sanskrit."

"And we have to be mindful of what the translations are in Sanskrit for each of these clues?"

"Maybe not all, but some of them," Mahesh argued.

Aarvi narrowed her eyes. "How do you figure that?"

"Look at the last phrase—*gratitude to the lord of death and peace*. That means you and me. Mahesh is the name for Shiv, the destroyer or lord of death. Aarvi, if my Sanskrit serves me right, means 'peace.' He is thanking you and me."

A smile spread across Aarvi's face. "Wow, I hadn't quite made that connection. I was still going down the list to see what the next one meant. That's quite impressive, Mahesh."

"Well, I wish I could take all the credit. But just as you recalled that the professor had an inclination for using Shakespearean English for clues, he also did the same for the names of gods and goddesses. That's what I recall from the college magazine."

"Whatever it might be, I think we are probably now on the right track," Aarvi acknowledged.

"Right. I did want to ask you something about the next one."

"The sentence about the aide? *His trusted aide was removed*?" Aarvi asked, looking at Mahesh.

"Yes. Remember, we heard from Rani yesterday that they have a new servant in the house. Do you recall anyone before that? Did the professor have someone who was the help before the new one joined?"

"Yes, he did! We saw him a couple of times when Devesh Uncle first moved back to Benares. This was before his accident. He used to accompany Devesh Uncle to the bookstore each time he came. I don't know what happened to him."

"I guess we can't ask Laxman or Rani without raising alarm bells," Mahesh claimed.

"No, but I think I know what the next sentence means. These sentences all seem to come in twos except that last one. My guess is the aide he was referring to now works at a club, since the next line says as much. Remember, Laxman and Rani said that Devesh Uncle was coming back from a club when he had his accident," Aarvi asserted.

"Yes, but which club?"

"Oh, that shouldn't be too difficult to figure out. We can ask Hari Uncle. Come to think of it, my father might know too. There aren't that many clubs here frequented by elderly people. I will ask him. If he doesn't know, then we will ask Hari Uncle," Aarvi responded, visibly pleased with herself.

Before they could continue, one of the store employees approached and told Aarvi to come downstairs. Mahesh followed them to where Tarun was seated. He was on the phone. Aarvi walked up to him, and he said something before handing her the phone. Mahesh waited a few steps away, browsing some books in a nearby aisle. Tarun looked at Mahesh and then approached him.

"Sorry, Mahesh. I needed Aarvi's help with something. One of our suppliers, you see. I don't have all the background," Tarun said.

"That's fine, sir. I am the one who should be thankful. It was very kind of you to let me visit the store and see everything it has to offer."

Tarun released a deep sigh, glancing around the store. "I don't know what I am going to do without her. I am not sure if she told you. She is getting married next weekend, and after that, running all this will once again fall on my shoulders."

"Yes, sir. She did tell me about the wedding. I didn't know she was moving away from Benares."

"No, she isn't. But once she is married, she won't be working here."

"Oh, I didn't know that," Mahesh said.

"Well, that's the way it works, you know. I knew this day would come. But I will certainly miss her. Do you like our store?"

"I love it, sir. It's brilliant. I love your collection upstairs. There's so much to see," Mahesh responded enthusiastically.

"Oh, I am glad you like it. It has been in our family for generations," Tarun said proudly. "I can't quite remember the exact quote, but I read somewhere that bookshops are a reminder that there are good things in the world."

"Vincent van Gogh, sir," Mahesh stated.

"You are right. Indeed, it is. Good to see that you read."

"Yes, sir. I love bookstores. I read somewhere that you are never really alone in a bookshop."

"Very true," Tarun agreed.

Before they could continue, Aarvi walked up to them. She spoke briefly with her father, handed him a document, and told him that the matter was taken care of. Then she asked him, "Did Devesh Uncle go to any club?"

"Yes. He was into yoga. There is a club near the university campus that he visited. You know, the one across from the main entrance," Tarun said, snapping his fingers as if trying to remember the name.

"You mean Om Yoga Center?" Aarvi asked.

"That's the one," Tarun replied.

A store clerk walked up to Tarun to have him sign some papers. He excused himself and headed back to his desk.

It was nearly 6:00 p.m. Aarvi explained to Mahesh that she had promised her mother that she would be home early that evening. "If you want, we can go to this yoga club tomorrow morning. It's a short walk from here. Around twenty minutes," she said.

"Sure," Mahesh replied. He felt a wave of dejection that they couldn't spend more time together and go to the club in the evening. From Aarvi's expression, it was apparent that she felt the same way.

They spoke for a few more minutes, agreeing on a time to meet at the bookstore the next morning. Before leaving, they walked over to Tarun's desk so that Mahesh could thank him. Tarun was on the phone again. Once he finished, he met Mahesh and Aarvi at the doorway.

"I guess you are leaving now?" Tarun asked Mahesh.

"Yes, sir."

"Well, thanks for stopping by and for your kind words about our establishment."

"The privilege is all mine."

"Before you go, I just remembered something about the Om Yoga Center and Devesh."

"Oh, what's that, sir?" Mahesh asked, and Aarvi shifted her gaze toward her father curiously.

"Laxman mentioned during Devesh's prayer ceremony that his servant is now working there. I have seen the fellow; I can't remember his name. But you remember, Aarvi, he came with Devesh to the store a few times," Tarun said.

"I remember him, but not his name," Aarvi replied. "Why is he working at the yoga club?"

"Laxman told me that he had to be let go after Devesh's accident. Rani and Laxman were pretty irked that he showed up at Devesh's condolence event."

Aarvi cocked her head, looking confused. Then she glanced at Mahesh before turning her gaze back at her father. "I'd have thought they would be happy he came since he worked with Devesh Uncle for such a long time."

"Yes, that he did. In fact, Devesh once mentioned in passing that he had been with him for nearly two decades, first in Delhi and then in Benares when they moved back," Tarun said thoughtfully, looking as if he was trying to remember something.

"Well, we can ask him tomorrow when we go visit the club," Aarvi said.

"Why the sudden interest in this fellow?" Tarun asked, looking between Mahesh and Aarvi. Before Mahesh could answer, Aarvi replied, "I will tell you in the evening after dinner."

Mahesh looked at Tarun and gave him a smile. He was about to turn and leave, and then he heard Tarun snapping his fingers.

"Yes, now I remember," Tarun revealed loudly. "Laxman told me that Devesh's servant had stolen something from their household. That's why they had to let him go. It seems there was some family heirloom that went missing, and Rani and Laxman were convinced that he was the culprit. I am guessing they didn't have enough to go to the police with, but they dismissed him anyway. And then…"

"Then what?" Aarvi demanded.

"Laxman had also mentioned that after Devesh's accident, the same servant wasn't giving him his medicines properly. He almost made it sound like this fellow didn't want Devesh to recover."

Book

Aarvi arrived home late, and Ritika was not happy about that. After getting an earful, Aarvi got down to arranging sarees and other gifts that needed to be distributed to guests at the wedding. But her mind was elsewhere. She was still thinking about the clues that Devesh had left.

Unfortunately, it took almost two hours to sort everything out. By the time they finished and sat down for dinner, they were both exhausted. Thankfully, Ashish had finished his meal and was back in his room, sparing them from any discussion about his grades, college admission, and future. They ate in silence, and once Ritika left, Tarun turned to Aarvi.

"Are you going to tell me what's going on? Why all the questions today about Devesh?"

Aarvi hesitated. "Do you remember the books and papers that I picked up from Laxman and Rani?"

"The ones he left for you and that boy, Mahesh."

"Well, it seems they are clues of some sort, and that's what we are trying to figure out."

"What sort of clues?" Tarun asked.

"We are not entirely sure yet," Aarvi replied, her words faltering. She didn't want to give her father all the details, which might trigger a prolonged conversation. If she divulged what she and Mahesh had uncovered so far, Tarun might get worried or, worse, ask them to stop searching for the truth. She knew from his face he wasn't satisfied with her answer, and he pressed further.

"So, these clues pointed to his servant working at a yoga club? That doesn't make any sense. Why would Devesh leave that sort of clue in crosswords?"

"As I said, that's not the only thing. There are other clues, and we haven't had a chance to decipher everything yet."

"Hmm." Tarun stroked his chin in thought.

She glanced up at him, noting the confused look on his face. He had probably been expecting more openness. It was uncharacteristic for Aarvi to withhold details from her father. His expression told her he knew that she had figured out more than she was letting on.

"I am heading back to my room. I am tired," Aarvi said as she got up.

"Sleep tight."

"Oh, by the way, I will be going to the yoga center tomorrow to follow up on what we found in Devesh Uncle's crosswords."

"With Mahesh?"

"Yes," replied Aarvi, leaving before Tarun could say another word. She wanted to get back to her room to start solving the clues again.

She carefully paged through all the papers in the folder, wondering if Mahesh was doing the same thing. She leafed through the pages and scrutinized the next two sentences.

The book of poems in heritage is meant for the sea.
She lives in the city of the mad king.

They simply didn't make any sense. She went back to the initial clues and the book that had the reference to words in the puzzle, trying to solve them again from the beginning. She came up with the same set of words and sentences. *If only I could discuss this with Mahesh,* she thought.

Her thoughts returned to the conversation she had had with Mahesh earlier about Sanskrit and English and tried to translate the sentences. Suddenly, it dawned on her. The professor could have been referring them to the bookstore. *Heritage* translated into *Sanskriti*, the name of the bookstore, but the rest of the sentence and the next one—if indeed there was a connection—made no sense. There were several books on poetry in the bookstore. Aarvi found no reference to which one the professor was alluding to. *Who was the mad king?*

The reference to the sea made even less sense. She racked her brain for another hour. Apart from the realization that the professor might have been referring to a book of poems in the bookstore, she came up with nothing. When she moved on to the next two sentences, she felt drained and fell asleep. Aarvi didn't even notice when Ritika gently came into her room, moved the papers from her bed to her desk, switched off the lights, and put a blanket on her.

* * *

Back at the guesthouse, Mahesh took a quick nap and waited for Karan. They had planned to have dinner together at one of the nearby restaurants, and Mahesh was looking forward to it. While waiting in his room, he went over Devesh's crosswords again, trying to make sense of them. He picked up his writing pad and was about to get started when he heard a knock on the door. He opened it, and Karan barged in with a big smile, giving him a tight hug.

After they exchanged some pleasantries, Karan noticed all the papers on the desk. "Still working away on the puzzles, I see?" He picked up some of the puzzles, sifting through them.

"Yep," Mahesh responded with a slight sigh.

"Did you make any progress on figuring out what they all mean?"

"I am not quite sure."

"Hmm." Karan peered at the pages, tilting his head.

"Take a look," Mahesh said, pointing Karan to the sheet with all the sentences. Karan's eyes darted back and forth as he read and reread them.

"Have you considered that it could all be just gibberish?"

Mahesh cracked a smile. "I don't think so."

"Maybe the professor went mad during his last days."

"Or he was trying to tell us something."

"Who is 'us'?" Karan asked.

"Me and Aarvi. As I told you, she received puzzles and other papers too. When she solved them, she found the same set of sentences," Mahesh asserted.

"This, I have to hear. Let's head over for dinner, and we can talk all about it."

"Sure," Mahesh said, following Karan out of the room and then down the stairs into the lobby.

Karan walked over to the reception and spoke to the employees. As Mahesh glanced around the lobby, he saw a few guests huddled together, poring over guidebooks and maps on the many spacious sofas. Karan's family had invested in modernizing the properties they owned, and Mahesh knew that Karan had a hand in directing all the changes to this guesthouse.

Once Karan returned, they exited the building, passed through the gates, and started walking to the restaurant a mile away. The streets were lively at this time of night, with tourists from the nearby hotels strolling to the banks of the Ganges to enjoy the evening breeze.

Once they reached the restaurant, they settled into a corner and ordered some food, then reminisced about their days in college. After an hour or so, their conversation shifted once again to Devesh. It was Karan who broached the subject.

"Oh, I forgot to tell you. When I asked around, I found someone who works as a manager in one of our family's guesthouses. Apparently, he knew Devesh in college and then lost touch when the professor moved to Delhi."

Mahesh leaned forward. "Anything interesting?"

"Only that Devesh was quite the character in college. He was a colorful fellow, it seems, and quite a riot in his batch."

"Hard to imagine," Mahesh commented.

"Yes, he was a laid-back fellow during our college days. But people do mellow with age and marriage."

"Well, it certainly seems to have done the trick with you," Mahesh teased. They both laughed.

"I haven't aged all that much, thank you. Regarding marriage, the professor never married, as far as I know."

"That's what I thought," Mahesh said.

"Although his classmate did say he was very popular among the girls in college, and Devesh created quite a scandal just before graduation," Karan said, leaning back into his chair.

"What scandal?" Mahesh asked.

"Not entirely sure. But it was with some girl he was dating. Then Devesh moved to Delhi and lost touch with his friends back here in Benares."

Mahesh shrugged. "That *was* more than three decades ago. Who knows what happened that far back?"

"True. Anyway, that's what I learned. I am not sure if it helps."

"We will see, but thanks. Any detail about the professor might come in handy," Mahesh acknowledged.

"Yeah, maybe you can discuss it with your good 'friend' Aarvi to see what she thinks," Karan said with a wink.

"Oh, come off it," Mahesh replied, ignoring the comment and turning his thoughts toward what they had learned so far.

Before they could continue, their food arrived. They paused for a few minutes till the waiter finished serving them. Once he left, they dived into their thalis.

"So, Aarvi was able to solve the puzzles as you did?" Karan asked, finishing off a mouthful of naan and dal.

Mahesh nodded. "She did."

"Smart girl."

"Yes, she is."

"Right," Karan said, raising his eyebrows playfully.

"Enough of this. Tell me, do you recall the professor having a love interest or relationship with anyone during his time in Delhi?"

"Not really," Karan responded.

"Hmm. This scandal you are referring to was probably with someone in Benares."

"Well, it *was* in college. What exactly are you getting at?" Karan continued.

"I'm thinking about the cryptic clues that the professor left us, the one that says, 'She lives in the city of the mad king.' It is possible he's referring to someone he was close to."

"Love interest?"

Mahesh furrowed his brow. "Maybe."

"It could be someone else from his time in Delhi."

"That is far more likely. He did live and work there for more than thirty years," Mahesh suggested.

They spent the next few minutes finishing off their thalis and lassi.

"You know," Karan said, gesturing at one of the waiters to bring the bill, "one thing I cannot get my head around is why he left clues for you and Aarvi."

A Poet's Ballad, A Crossword Mystery

"We are good at crossword puzzles," said Mahesh.

"I think there's probably more to it than that," Karan maintained.

"Like what?"

Karan lifted his shoulders. "Don't know. There are other people who are good at solving puzzles. Maybe not as good as the two of you. Still, I find it odd that he would leave these for you and Aarvi. You didn't know him that well. I think there's still something missing."

"Well, he did leave other things, mostly books for his other students."

"Yes, but not puzzles." Karan gave him a pointed look.

"Not that I know of."

"Well, I don't know. It's all rather mysterious. Anyway, you don't have much time, do you? To figure this all out, I mean. You are leaving on Sunday morning, and tomorrow is Wednesday."

"That's right," Mahesh said thoughtfully.

After settling their bill, Mahesh and Karan walked back to the guesthouse. They stopped at a roadside stall to have some tea and chatted about Karan's family business, Mahesh's college in London, and some mutual friends. After walking Mahesh back, Karan bade him goodnight.

Mahesh trudged up the stairs to his room. He settled into bed, picked up the file from Devesh, and started looking through all the papers again to see if he had indeed missed anything.

* * *

Mahesh had agreed to meet Aarvi at the bookstore around 10:00 a.m. He was there at 9:00 a.m. and took pictures of the area, the ghat, and the famous narrow lanes of Benares. His mother had told him about her college days in the city, and they had visited Benares a few years ago. It was one of the few family vacations he had enjoyed, well before his siblings had become involved in the family business. Back then, things had been less complicated.

Mahesh was astounded by how much things had changed in this old city. It was more crowded, hosting many more foreign tourists, hotels, and guesthouses. On the other hand, the narrow lanes, old houses, temples, monuments, and riverbank still looked the same. Mahesh spent a good hour taking pictures before heading to the bookstore. He was looking forward to meeting Aarvi.

He found her waiting at the entrance, looking radiant as ever. Tarun, stationed at his usual spot near the cashier's desk, gave him a gentle nod and a smile.

Mahesh and Aarvi walked to the back of the store and up the stairs. They sat across a small desk on the upper floor, and an employee promptly brought them some tea. After talking about the pictures that Mahesh had been taking, they dived into the subject of Devesh and his puzzles. Mahesh filled Aarvi in on what Karan had said about Devesh and his college days.

Aarvi wrapped her hands around her teacup. "I could ask my father, too. He knew Devesh Uncle well during his time in BHU, although they grew apart once he left for Delhi."

"You think he might tell us something that could help?" Mahesh asked.

"I don't know. Honestly, I'm not sure whether I want to talk to him more about this."

"You mean your father? Why?"

"I am not entirely sure he likes what we are up to, and if he tells my mother, it would be a total catastrophe," Aarvi said with a sigh.

"Oh?"

"She just wants me to focus on my wedding next weekend and nothing else. She doesn't like me spending time at the store. If she knew that I was chasing all this, she would throw a fit."

"Well, let's not get you into trouble, then. If you don't want to follow up on the clues, I can do it myself and will let you know how things go," Mahesh offered.

"No," Aarvi said in a stern voice that surprised him.

"What do you mean?"

"Devesh Uncle left clues for *both* of us. I am part of it too, whether you like it or not."

"I love it, totally. You are terrific, and I'm enjoying all this because of you, more than anything else," Mahesh said, making Aarvi blush slightly.

"Well, that's settled then," Aarvi said with a degree of finality. "First stop is the yoga center to find out more from Devesh Uncle's servant, who works there."

"Sounds like a plan. Do you think his servant might be responsible, I mean, for the professor's death? The clues did point us to him," Mahesh declared.

"True, I was thinking about that. I mean, it is possible, I guess. The problem is we can't ask him directly about that or else he might get defensive and not answer any questions."

Mahesh nodded. They finished their tea, and after chatting a bit more, they decided to make their way to the yoga club. It was a good twenty-minute walk from the bookstore, the shortest route being a path along the Ganges. As they strolled down the riverbank, they could see boats filled with tourists floating past. The bright morning sun glimmering on the river made it look like a painting.

The club wasn't busy. The old, run-down building featured a spacious hall on the ground floor. On each side of the building were some ill-maintained lawns, where a few members were practicing asanas with their instructors. Walking up to a small booth that looked like a reception near the main entrance, they approached the old gentleman seated there with a newspaper. Once they told him they were looking for Professor Devesh Tripathi's help, he obliged right away and asked one of the nearby instructors to fetch someone named Kulwant.

While they waited, the gentleman spoke fondly of Devesh. He didn't seem to know much about Devesh's personal life apart from his love for yoga and that he attended poetry readings. The man said the professor had visited the club often when he had first moved back to Benares, but after his accident, he had stopped coming altogether. Before long, Aarvi and Mahesh turned around to see another older gentleman standing beside them.

He said, "Namaste, I am Kulwant. I worked in the professor's household in Delhi and Benares."

"Yes, thank you for meeting us," Mahesh said politely, and Aarvi nodded. "This will only take a few minutes. We'd like to talk to you about the professor. Can we perhaps talk near the gate or over there?" Mahesh pointed to an empty corner near one of the lawns.

"I am on a break. Let's go outside, and we can talk for a few minutes."

"Sure."

Aarvi and Mahesh followed Kulwant out of the club gates until they reached a nearby tea stall. They ordered tea and found a spot beneath the shade of a tree, out of earshot of the other patrons.

"What's this about? Have Rani and Laxman said anything about me?" Kulwant demanded in a loud voice.

Mahesh held up his hands in a reassuring gesture. "Oh no. You don't have to worry. They don't know we are here. We just wanted to talk about the professor. You see, he left us some puzzles and papers, and we are trying to make sense of it all."

Kulwant's eyes carried a wistful sparkle. "Yes. Students, puzzles, and poems—they were his life. What do you want to know?"

"We are aware you left the Tripathi residence after the professor's accident—"

"I didn't leave," Kulwant cut in. "I was let go. Laxman and Rani made sure of that. They accused me of stealing.

Can you believe that?" he huffed, sitting back with a scowl.

"Stealing what?"

"Jewelry and watches. Tell me, what would an old man like me do with those things? The professor was my family. I had been with him for twenty years. Why on earth would I steal anything? They just wanted me out of the house," Kulwant said, raising his voice.

Aarvi spoke next in a gentler, less inquisitive tone. "We are not here to accuse you of anything, and we do believe you," she said.

The tea arrived, and they paused to take a few sips before Aarvi continued. "Did the professor ever tell you anything that would suggest that his life was in danger?"

"You mean the accident?"

She nodded.

"Well, I was let go a week after it happened. It was a strange accident. He was returning from the club in the evening. While he was walking back from the bus stop, a lorry hit him. He was lucky to be alive," Kulwant noted solemnly.

"Why was it strange?" Aarvi asked.

"Well, it's a residential neighborhood, and the area around the bus stop is well lit. It's a quiet area not frequented by lorries, so it surprised me. The consensus was that it was a drunk driver."

"But you are not convinced?" Aarvi asked.

"It's not that. I didn't think much of it. But when the professor came home after a few days at the hospital, he hinted that his mishap was deliberate and wanted the police to investigate it," Kulwant went on.

Aarvi's eyes widened. "Did they? I mean, did the police follow up on it?"

"I believe they did. I don't know all the details. After that, Rani and Laxman got rid of me based on their trumped-up charges. They prevented me from even visiting or talking to the professor. I tried to see if I could get into his room since it is on the ground floor, but then I noticed they had moved him upstairs."

"Do you really think that the professor's accident and death were not natural? Don't worry. This stays between us," Mahesh said, choosing his words carefully.

"My gut feeling is that something is not right. I know that the police investigated and found no evidence of wrongdoing. My cousin is a constable at the station where the report was filed by one of the professor's friends, Hari Das. Nothing happened after that," Kulwant stated. Before Aarvi or Mahesh could ask anything, Kulwant continued, "some friend he is." The tone in his voice startled Aarvi and Mahesh.

"What do you mean?" Mahesh asked. "I mean what you were saying about Hari."

"Where was Hari babu when the Devesh babu was alive? He had asked me to go and get Hari babu not once but twice after his accident. He had sent him two letters. But Hari babu never showed up," Kulwant scoffed.

"But I thought…," Mahesh started but was interrupted immediately.

"Only when Devesh babu died did Hari babu wake up and start creating all sorts of noise," Kulwant huffed. Mahesh and Aarvi looked at each other. They had never considered Hari to be involved in the professor's death. After all, it was Hari who had contacted them and insisted that they visit Devesh's residence to pick up what was left for them. However, Kulwant's commentary was shedding a different light on Hari Das.

Aarvi joined in. "The professor's room was on the ground floor, and it also had a phone, right?"

"Yes. There's only one telephone, and it's on that floor," Kulwant confirmed.

"Hmm." Aarvi sipped her tea, looking thoughtful.

"Once they moved him upstairs, there wasn't much he could do. From what I heard, his movements were severely restricted. He was such a nice man, and it is wrong that something like this happened to him," Kulwant added sadly. "And then that doctor…"

"What doctor?" Aarvi pressed.

"Didn't they tell you?"

"No," Aarvi said, shaking her head, gesturing Kulwant to continue.

"They changed his doctor. They found this young doctor who was a tenant before to treat Devesh babu. They got rid of the doctor that had been assigned by the hospital, whom the professor trusted and replaced him with this new doctor," Kulwant said.

"I am sorry. I am a bit lost. What do you mean, the doctor who was a tenant?" Aarvi demanded.

"While the professor was away in Delhi, Laxman decided to rent out his room to a young doctor. Devesh babu was not aware of this and when he found out, he was livid. Anyhow, they got this same fellow to treat him after his accident. I never trusted that fellow," Kulwant divulged.

"What's his name? Where is this doctor now?" Aarvi asked.

"I don't know. They never shared those details with me. But I never saw him again after Devesh babu passed away," Kulwant responded, shaking his head.

Mahesh and Aarvi could see that he was getting emotional and gave him some time to gather his thoughts. Aarvi glanced sideways at Mahesh and, after a long minute, decided to ask Kulwant something.

"I know you are angry with the way Rani and Laxman treated you. But before the accident, did they treat the professor right? Were they nice to him?"

"Not exactly. You must understand that they were living in the house by themselves before he moved back to Benares. It's a joint property, and it did affect their privacy. I overheard them talking a few times about wanting to leave, but it didn't happen."

"Do you know why? If it bothered them so much, why didn't they move out?" Aarvi asked.

"Well, for one, it's their house, too. I think they probably would have moved into another house if they could have afforded it," Kulwant noted.

"Are they not well off? From what I know, Laxman has his own business."

"They are. But I heard that Laxman wanted to invest in more properties. There were many discussions and arguments between them about money. Who knows? Maybe they needed money, and Devesh babu wasn't willing to give them anything. I do know they wanted to sell the house, and he refused. I think they found him to be a nuisance."

"Was he scared of them?" Mahesh butted in.

The question seemed to take Kulwant by surprise. "I think after the accident, he probably was. If he suspected them of trying to harm him, I am sure he was scared," he replied.

"But you are not convinced," pressed Mahesh.

Kulwant paused and seemed to ponder before responding. "I can't say for sure. But Devesh babu did give me a sealed document to take to his lawyer. I didn't ask him about it. I suspect he wanted to change his will, but never got around to it. These are family affairs, and I didn't get to talk to him about it."

"Who is the lawyer that you gave the sealed document to?"

"Mangal Kumar. He lives near Ramnagar Fort. But I was told that he was away on a long trip abroad to visit his son. I left the document with his clerk, and I am not sure what happened after that."

Mahesh felt a pit in his stomach. "Did Laxman and Rani know about this?"

"About the sealed document?"

"Yes."

"Perhaps. I am not sure. The professor categorically told me not to mention it to them. I had to sneak it out of the house. After I delivered it to the lawyer, the professor told me to then keep an eye out in case Mangal Kumar came to visit him. But I was let go right after that."

"So, you don't know if Mangal Kumar ever got around to visiting or contacting him?" Mahesh inquired.

"No," Kulwant sighed despondently. "It's so sad that I wasn't with him during the time he needed me most. I am convinced of one thing: Laxman and Rani wanted to get rid of me so that the professor couldn't tell me what he suspected. They knew he trusted me, and I would always look out for him, try my best to keep him safe."

Mahesh fiddled anxiously with his cup. "Do you know where Mangal Kumar lives, where his offices are?"

"His offices are in the main courthouse," Kulwant replied.

Before he could say anything further, Aarvi stepped in. "I know where that is." She swung around to face Mahesh. "It shouldn't be difficult to find him."

They finished their tea, and after a few minutes, Kulwant said he needed to head back to the club. Before parting ways, Mahesh approached him once more.

"You have been most helpful, Kulwant. Before you go, I have one last question. As far as we know, the professor was unmarried. Did he have any love interest or special friend, so to say?"

A smile spread across Kulwant's face. "He had friends, most of whom were colleagues from Delhi University. But he always spoke fondly of his college days here in Benares. I often asked him why he never got married. He mentioned something about a love interest in college that never panned out. I don't know the details. But when he did reminisce, he always referred to her as the one that got away."

"Any idea who that might have been?" Mahesh prodded.

"None whatsoever. This was well before I started working for him. The only thing I know is that he always wore a sad smile when he spoke of that time."

"Thank you, Kulwant. You have helped immensely."

Once Kulwant left, Aarvi looked at Mahesh. "He believes the same thing as Hari Uncle, but Kulwant seems to suggest that Laxman and Rani had a hand in both the accident *and* the professor's death. He also points a finger at Hari Uncle and suspects this doctor."

"So it would seem." Mahesh nodded with a sigh.

"What are we supposed to do with all this? The police are already aware. Do you think Hari Uncle might be responsible?"

"I mean Hari Das has an eccentric personality and his quirkiness does lend himself to be someone who could do this. I don't know him well enough to know whether he is capable of this. But then why would he get us involved and have us chase all this? It doesn't make sense," Mahesh said.

"What are we supposed to do with all this?" Aarvi said, waving her arms.

"Let's solve the rest of the puzzles and see where those lead," Mahesh suggested.

Aarvi nodded gently as Mahesh paid for their tea.

They began their stroll back to the bookstore, and Aarvi took Mahesh on a different, longer route, which allowed them to talk more. They meandered down a lane filled with open-air stores selling souvenirs. It wasn't too crowded, so they could walk side by side. Aarvi stopped at a store with large glass windows and peered at the handicrafts inside.

"Do you know what those are?" Aarvi asked, pointing to some notebooks with covers featuring beautiful, intricate designs.

"Filigree, isn't it?"

"Yes. I am impressed. Most people don't know what that is," Aarvi said with a smile. "I love them. I wanted to keep some in our store, but my father refused because they are overpriced. But they are so beautiful. If you had them, you would be compelled to write and then come back and read every now and then."

"Do you?"

"What?"

"Write? Do you have any notebooks?" Mahesh asked.

"No, I don't have any of these ones. They are expensive, and they're mostly for people who are interested in writing their memoirs or stories."

"You didn't answer my first question," Mahesh said, fixing his gaze on Aarvi.

Her smile widened. "I have dabbled in short stories, but nothing too serious. I am not sure whether people would even like them."

"Who cares? You can do it because you like it."

"True, but what good are stories if people don't read them?"

"You can write them for yourself. Some people will like it, and some won't. They will still be yours. Plus, you can always go back to them. I had a friend in school who used to write, and many people didn't like what he wrote. I asked him whether it bothered him. He said that when he is writing, he is on a journey with his imagination, and he loves every minute of it. For him, that in itself is rewarding," Mahesh said.

"Good point. I guess I am still a bit shy about sharing what I've written and worried about what people might think," Aarvi conveyed.

Mahesh saw that Aarvi's gaze had fixated on a beautiful filigree notebook. Then she tore her eyes away, and they resumed their walk toward the bookshop.

"Can I ask you something about the other sentences?" Mahesh glanced at her.

"Sure. Actually, I do have a theory on the one that says, 'The book of poems in heritage is meant for the sea.'"

"Oh, that's what I was going to talk about. Please, go ahead. Let's hear your thoughts first," Mahesh said.

"Well, I think it refers to a book of poems in our store. The name of the store, Sanskriti, translates to 'heritage,'" Aarvi said thoughtfully. "I don't know what the rest of the sentence means."

"Hmm. I think you may be right. However, I don't think it's a book of published poems that he is referring to."

"What do you mean?"

"The professor was an amateur poet. We knew that in college, he went to poetry readings and Kavi Sammelans," Mahesh declared.

"You mean poetry festivals?"

"Yes."

"His poems, were they any good?" Aarvi asked.

"I don't know. I read a few that he had brought once to the Scrabble club in college. Honestly, I don't remember if they were any good. I am not into poetry, so I really wouldn't know."

"Well, neither am I. But if it's a good poem, it will appeal to folks who are not into poetry as well."

"True," Mahesh said, smiling.

"Coming back to what you were saying, if it's not a book in the store, then what exactly are you thinking?" Aarvi prodded.

"Right. So, when I read the clue, my thought was that he left a book of his own poems in the store somewhere."

Aarvi shook her head. "That's unlikely. One of the employees would have discovered it. We take an inventory of all the shelves each week, and a handwritten notebook would have stood out."

"You are probably right. I didn't think of that." Mahesh nodded slowly.

"Unless . . ." Aarvi stopped abruptly. A tourist almost bumped into Mahesh from behind. He apologized, and they edged to one side of the sidewalk where they could stop to talk.

"Unless what?" Mahesh locked his eyes on Aarvi, who seemed lost in thought.

"Unless he left it in the section where we keep the rare books. We only open that on special occasions, and we only take inventory of that section before and after each event."

"So, you think it's there, in that locked section?"

"Yes, now I remember. During the last annual event a few months ago, Devesh Uncle attended and spent a lot of time there. Rani and Laxman were with him the whole time. Maybe he just had enough time to sneak in a book without arousing their suspicion."

"Wouldn't it be easier to sneak in a letter?" asked Mahesh.

"Maybe, but think about it. It's possible that Rani and Laxman had been checking everything he was writing and carrying. A book wouldn't raise any questions. He could have easily picked up a book from the collection, browsed it, and then left his book alongside it when he was putting it back," Aarvi professed.

"Yes, and even if Laxman and Rani checked, they would have only found a notebook full of poems. He probably didn't want to take a chance with a letter."

"I mean, it's clear from everything we have seen and heard that the professor was scared of Laxman and Rani," Aarvi asserted.

"Exactly," Mahesh nodded. "I guess the next stop is the upper-floor collection in the bookstore to see if he really did leave a book of poems there."

"Right," Aarvi said.

They started walking again. The bright sun was now bearing down on the sidewalk, and the heat was taking its toll. They stopped at one of the numerous street-corner tobacco and soft-drink stalls for a Fanta.

"By the way, I am not sure whether you did so already, but I have figured out what the next sentence might be referring to," Mahesh said before taking a sip from his soda bottle.

"You mean the one that says, 'She lives in the city of the mad king.'" Aarvi gulped down almost half her bottle at once.

"Yes, that one."

"He was referring to someone living in a city where there used to be a mad king."

"Right. Did you figure out what that means?" Mahesh asked.

"No. I was thinking if we first made sense of the sentence before it, the next clue might become clearer."

"You are on the right track. The city of the mad king is Jaunpur. Do you know it?"

Aarvi scrunched her eyebrows. "Sure. Everyone in Benares knows of Jaunpur. It's a little over two hundred kilometers north of here toward Lucknow. I've been there a few times to meet with a stationery supplier. It's an industrial town but not particularly famous. There are a few monuments and a fort, but it doesn't get much by way of tourists. What does Jaunpur have to do with the mad king?" she asked as she finished her drink.

"The town is named after Jauna Khan, better known as Muhammad bin Tughlaq."

"You mean the sultan of Delhi in the mid-fourteenth century?" Aarvi asked.

"Yes. I am impressed. The one and the same. He was the ruler of the sultanate in the early part of the fourteenth century."

Aarvi tilted her head to one side. "What's the connection with the mad king?"

"Well, he was called the mad king because he wanted to move the capital from Delhi to Daulatabad, a city in present-day Maharashtra."

"Yeah, I recall reading something about that. But rulers change capitals all the time. What was so mad about that?" she asked.

"That's the thing. This guy didn't just move the capital—he wanted to move the entire population of Delhi to Daulatabad."

Aarvi raised her eyebrows. "Wow."

"Not only that, but he even wanted to move all the animals in Delhi to the new capital. There was a special road constructed to facilitate the migration. Of course, the entire exercise failed spectacularly, with many people dying during the journey."

Aarvi shook her head. "Unbelievable."

Mahesh shrugged. "Yeah, well, he was, like all rulers from that era, a tyrant. Historians have a mixed opinion of him. Some have suggested that he was educated and showed interest in medicine, science, and philosophy. He also instituted token currency, which once again failed for many reasons."

"So there is some connection to Jaunpur in all of this?"

Mahesh nodded. "That's what I think."

"It's a good thing I have a historian with me," Aarvi said in a teasing voice.

Mahesh laughed. After finishing his drink, he handed the soda bottle back to the street vendor, and they resumed their walk to the store.

* * *

Once they were back inside, Aarvi rushed to one of the little rooms behind the cashier's desk and brought out a large set of keys. She had asked Mahesh to wait near the staircase.

Tarun, who was talking to some customers as usual, spotted his daughter dashing through the store. When he saw her scurrying by with a set of keys to the section upstairs, he wore a pensive expression.

He is surely wondering what is going on, Aarvi thought. From the corner of her eye, she noticed Tarun watching them as they headed upstairs.

The collection behind the locked door was divided into four small aisles. Aarvi and Mahesh started on different ends, searching for Devesh's notebook. They figured it wouldn't be hard to locate. The rest of the books were neatly arranged and nicely bound. The notebook would stand out unless it was well hidden.

Once they reached the third aisle, Aarvi slowed down. Remembering something, she fixed her gaze on one shelf. "Devesh Uncle was tired and was sitting here on a chair while browsing the books in this section. I am sure it's here somewhere."

Together, they removed each book, peeking behind each stack in search of the notebook. Their excitement was giving way to frustration. Aarvi wondered if they had gotten it all wrong.

"No, you are right, Aarvi. I am confident we are on the right track. The notebook *must* be here somewhere. Let's just keep looking."

"Right," Aarvi said, regaining some of her enthusiasm.

Mahesh's fingers hovered over the spines. He paused in front of a row of older-looking books. One of them was not aligned properly. He slowly took it out. Behind it was a gray notebook. He carefully brought it out and showed it to Aarvi, who was standing close enough to feel his breath.

"I think this is it," Mahesh said in a low but sure voice.

A Poet's Ballad, A Crossword Mystery

Aarvi smiled as she eyed the small notebook. "Yes!"

They found the nearest reading desk and stood side by side as they started paging through the thin notebook. It contained around fifty pages filled with neatly handwritten poems. *Devesh Uncle must have written them over many years,* Aarvi thought. He had used different pens, and the yellowed pages showed signs of wear and tear. Devesh had taken pains to put a cover on the notebook, and it was evident from the writing that it had meant a lot to him.

The hundred-odd poems that filled the notebook were in different languages, most in Hindi and a few in Sanskrit and English. Aarvi and Mahesh spent the next two hours scrutinizing each page, taking a few breaks in between and marveling at Devesh's use of language. Although neither of them was into poetry, they were impressed. One thing that was abundantly clear—nearly all the poems were about love. He had poured his heart into them.

"He was in love," Mahesh said as he slowly turned the last page in the book and closed it.

"Yes," Aarvi replied. "These were meant for someone."

"The woman of the sea. Remember the puzzle," Mahesh said.

"Of course. I wonder who that is or was?"

"It's not clear from the book, and the titles don't have any names. I am sure her name is hidden in one of the passages or poems, but it will take us forever to figure it out."

"Why didn't he consider publishing them? I mean, these are clearly good enough to be published," Aarvi wondered aloud.

"As you said, he wrote them for himself, and they were meant for someone specific."

"Right," Aarvi nodded. She picked up the book again and started poring over the cover and back pages to see if there were any other clues.

Mahesh sighed. "Outside his family, I can only think of two people in the professor's life who go far back enough that we could ask."

"I know," Aarvi said, still leafing through the notebook. "My father and Hari Uncle."

"Who knew him better?"

"Hari Uncle, I'd imagine. I can't ask my father about this. He knew him but never really spoke much about him."

"Can we ask Hari then?" Mahesh asked.

"No harm in trying. I will call him to see if he's home. We can grab some lunch and then head over to his house," Aarvi suggested.

"Sure. You don't have any work at the store?"

"I do, but this is so much more interesting," Aarvi replied. She had never thought that she would ever find something more exciting than spending time at the store. She knew it was not just because of the puzzles, but also because of Mahesh. She wondered whether he knew that was the case.

Aarvi locked up the rare books section and made her way down the stairs, Mahesh following behind. Before heading out, they stopped briefly to speak to Tarun.

Aarvi didn't want to tell him everything they had learned about Devesh. Mahesh was carrying the book of poems in his satchel, and Aarvi made no mention of it. Tarun pressed his daughter for more details, but she only gave him vague answers.

Tarun then told Aarvi that her mother had called to remind her that Jeev's family was coming over for dinner in the evening and that she had to be back home early. Aarvi had completely forgotten about that, but she didn't tell her father as much. Ritika had made it clear that it would be rude and embarrassing if she showed up after her future in-laws had arrived. Aarvi promised to be back on time. Mahesh, as always, was polite during the entire conversation.

After a quick lunch, they reached Hari's residence. It was already late afternoon by the time they arrived. A servant let them in and asked them to wait. They sat down together on the sofa, recalling Hari's instructions during their previous visit. The memory made Aarvi smile as they waited for him.

After a few minutes, Hari stepped into the room and sat across from them in an armchair. He instructed his servant to bring some juice and water, which were soon placed on the coffee table.

"I am sorry. I was taking a nap. It's so hot nowadays that there isn't much one can do in this weather except sleep," Hari said, helping himself to a glass of water.

"Thank you for seeing us on such a short notice," Aarvi said, and Mahesh nodded gently.

"Not a problem. So, what is it you want to talk about?"

"As you know, Hari Uncle, we picked up what the professor had left for us. It was mostly books and some crossword puzzles."

"What kind of puzzles? I'd have thought Devesh would have left you something of importance," Hari pronounced.

"Well, we are still trying to figure that out," Aarvi replied, casting a sideways glance at Mahesh. They had decided not to let Hari know everything lest he contact the police based on the clues alone with no evidence to back up their assertions.

"Hmm, that's odd. I knew Devesh quite well in college, you know. Tarun too," Hari said, looking at Aarvi. "Then life happened, and we all got busy. Devesh moved away and we lost touch. Best days of our lives, I tell you."

"Before we get to his past, can I ask you something else?"

"What's on your mind?" Hari asked, gazing at Mahesh and then Aarvi with a curious look on his face.

"Do you know if the professor had a will?" Aarvi asked.

"No, he never spoke to me about it. Why?" demanded Hari.

"Well, we visited Kulwant earlier today," Aarvi continued.

"Kulwant? Ah yes. His servant for many years."

"He works at a yoga center now. Laxman and Rani let him go after Devesh Uncle's accident."

"What's that got to do with the will?" pressed Hari.

"Kulwant told us that Devesh Uncle had given him a letter in a sealed envelope that had to be delivered to Mangal Kumar, a lawyer. We can only imagine that it must be a will or a document of some relevance. He also said that Laxman and Rani should not be told about this."

"I knew it! Those scoundrels!" Hari exclaimed, banging his palm on the chair. Aarvi and Mahesh were taken aback by his sudden change in demeanor.

"Unfortunately, it seems Mangal Kumar is on an extended hiatus abroad to visit his son. Kulwant left it with his clerk, and then he was let go. We don't know if Mr. Kumar saw the document or tried to contact Devesh Uncle before he passed away," Aarvi continued.

"Now that is strange," Hari said, drumming his fingers on his armrest.

"What?" Aarvi asked.

"Mangal is away now but was very much in town till only a while ago. So why did Kulwant leave the document with his clerk? Unless…"

"Unless what?" Aarvi and Mahesh asked hurriedly in unison, leaning forward.

"Unless Kulwant didn't give the document to the clerk, or maybe the clerk didn't let Mangal know of its existence. Ha! That must be it!"

"What?" demanded Aarvi, sitting at the edge of the sofa.

"I remember Mangal telling me that his clerk used to work for Laxman's company before. There has to be a connection. Don't worry. I know Mangal. He is expected back next month. I will get to the bottom of this. I am sure Devesh changed his will. He had a premonition of what was going to happen and didn't want to leave anything to his wretched relatives," Hari alleged.

"We are not sure of that. This is just what we are assuming," Aarvi said, not wanting Hari to jump to conclusions and start writing letters to everyone.

Hari suddenly became quiet, lost in thought. Aarvi and Mahesh looked at each other, wondering whether they should snap him out of it. After a moment, he looked at them and smiled.

"I am proud of both of you. You have done good work. I knew that there was a reason Devesh selected the two of you. Don't worry about the will. I'll pay a visit to Mangal's office tomorrow and find out more."

"Thank you, Uncle," Aarvi replied.

"Now, you said you wanted me to tell you about Devesh's past. What do you want to know?"

Aarvi watched Mahesh from the corner of her eye, expecting him to ask Hari about the rest.

"Well, sir, we were hoping you could tell us something about him during his college days," Mahesh started.

"That's a long time ago. I don't remember everything, but I can certainly try," Hari said in a more relaxed voice.

"Was he popular?"

"In what sense?"

"I-I-I mean w-w-with . . ." Mahesh stuttered.

"You mean with girls? Yes, he certainly was," Hari said with a smirk.

"Was he romantically involved with anyone?" Mahesh continued in a slightly subdued tone.

"Ah, I see what you are getting at. I am guessing there was something in the puzzles or the material that he left both of you?"

"That's what we are trying to figure out, Hari Uncle," Aarvi replied without getting into specifics.

Hari leaned back into his armchair, closed his eyes, and suddenly smiled brightly. Then he opened his eyes. "Yes, there was someone. It was a long, long time ago."

"What happened?" Mahesh asked.

"Devesh went out with a girl for almost a year and a half, and things were really serious during the final year before graduation. It was common knowledge that they would marry. What we didn't know was that the girl's family was not aware of their relationship. Remember, this was back in the late forties, early fifties. It was a different India back then. It was rare for boys and girls to go against the wishes of their parents."

"But from what I know, sir, he was single," Mahesh said.

"That's right. You see, the girl's family was up in arms when they found out. It didn't work out in the end.

Devesh was heartbroken, and I believe that was one of the reasons he left Benares and moved to Delhi."

"What happened to the girl?" Aarvi asked.

"Apparently, her romance with Devesh caused more of a scandal in her family than we'd thought. One day, we learned that her parents had taken her back home. She didn't even get to graduate. Imagine that! They could have at least let the poor girl write her exams and get her degree. But two months before graduation, she left—or, rather, was made to leave. Then we heard that her parents married her off in a hurry a month later. None of her friends from college were invited. We found out much, much later. Such a shame. I tell you, even within the educated class, women don't get a fair shake in this country, even after three decades," Hari said.

"I have to agree," Mahesh said. Aarvi kept quiet, not knowing how to respond.

"Does that help you in any way?" Hari asked, looking at Mahesh since Aarvi had become more withdrawn.

"Do you know where she is now?"

"No, we lost touch after that. With her family coming down hard on her, it was clear that keeping any contact with her would be complicated."

"So, the last time you saw her was in college?" Mahesh asked.

"Yes," Hari responded with a sigh, leaning back into his chair.

"No news of her since then?" Mahesh pressed.

"A couple of years ago, I ran into one of our mutual friends who was visiting Benares. He told me that she is married, and is now Mrs. Kapoor, and has a daughter. She is well settled in her hometown. That's all I know."

"Did the professor know all this?"

"I don't think he'd had any contact with her after college. He told me as much. When I mentioned my chance meeting with this friend and what he'd said, he seemed unfazed. Decades had passed since college, and these things happen. People move on, and that's it."

"What was her name, and where was she from?" Mahesh asked.

"Oh, I should have mentioned that. Her name is Mira, and she is from Jaunpur."

Aarvi and Mahesh locked eyes. He was right about the connection to Jaunpur. Thanks to Hari, they had also figured out the connection to the sea. *Mira* translated to *the ocean* in Sanskrit. The book of poems that Professor Devesh Tripathi had left in the Sanskriti Bookshop was meant for Mira Kapoor from Jaunpur.

Woman

The visit to Hari Das's house left Aarvi and Mahesh craving answers. Fortunately, they now knew whom Devesh had wanted to leave the book of poems to. Hari made a few calls to his extended family in Jaunpur, and after an hour or so, one of them was able to share Mira Kapoor's address. The acquaintance whom Hari spoke with did not have her phone number, nor did he know Mira personally.

It was evident that Hari was happy with what Aarvi and Mahesh had uncovered. What worried Aarvi was whether he would start pestering the police about investigating Devesh's death based on their findings. They did appreciate his offer to follow up with the lawyer regarding the document that Devesh had sent him.

Toward the end of the conversation, Hari had become quiet, casting curious glances at Aarvi. It was almost as if he wanted to ask or tell her something but couldn't with Mahesh there. Aarvi guessed as much, but the excitement of their new discovery dominated their entire conversation once they left Hari's residence. They stopped at a small tea shop on the banks of the Ganges, sitting down on a wooden bench beneath the shade of a towering banyan tree to have some sweet lassis.

The banks of the majestic river were slowly filling up with pilgrims and tourists. The sun was now setting, and although it was still hot, a gentle breeze made the weather more bearable. The sky glowed red, reflecting on the water until it sparkled with an orange hue, unlike the morning sun that had tinged the river with a mix of blue, gray, and white. Some eager photographers were trying to capture the moment through the arches of various buildings and monuments that lined the river.

Aarvi and Mahesh sat silently for a few minutes, enjoying their drinks and soaking in the scenery around them. Finally, Aarvi broke the silence. "We have to give the book to Mira," she declared.

"Yes. I was planning to go to Jaunpur tomorrow and hand it over to her. I have to check with Karan to see if

I can still use the car for the trip. If not, I will rent one from the guesthouse for the day," Mahesh said.

"Are you going to meet Karan tonight?"

He nodded. "He has invited me over to his house to meet his family. I can ask him about Laxman too. He mentioned that one of the guesthouse managers used to work in the property firm that Laxman partly owns. I might get some more details from him, although I'm not sure how much it will help."

"Mm-hmm," Aarvi said, her mind drifting.

"Are you all right?" Mahesh asked with a worried look.

"Yes. Well, I mean . . ."

"Do you want to come with me to Jaunpur for the day? We would come back in the evening. I know it may be tricky for you, but I'd love for you to join me."

"I want to go . . ."

"Great. It's settled then," Mahesh said happily.

"Not quite, Mahesh," Aarvi murmured. She had never really called him by his name.

His smile fell. "What is it?"

"It's not that simple. If I tell my parents that I'm going to Jaunpur with you, they will ask me all sorts of questions. I am not sure what to tell them."

"How about the truth?"

"I doubt they would be too happy about that," Aarvi said.

"But they would understand that we are going to hand over a book that the professor left for a friend."

"No, they wouldn't," Aarvi stated, looking away. There was a lull in their conversation.

"We could both ask your father when we go back to the store."

"No, he is not the problem. Let me deal with him. Maybe I will tell them that I am meeting a supplier in Jaunpur. That might work."

"Have you done that before? I mean, gone to Jaunpur to meet a supplier."

"Yes, I told you, remember? Anyway, let me think about it. I really do want to go," Aarvi asserted.

"Okay. Well, if I can help in any way, please let me know," Mahesh offered.

"Well, you are the problem, you see," Aarvi said, her tone lightening as a smile tugged at her lips.

"Oh," Mahesh replied, glancing away awkwardly.

"Don't worry, I am just teasing you. I'm not sure if I can make you understand. I am getting married next weekend. Both my family and my in-laws are conservative. If I tell them I am going off with a strange young man to a town four hours away for the entire day, there will be *lots* of questions."

"Ah, I see."

"To top it all off, the reason for going is to hand over a book of poems written by a professor to his love interest," Aarvi added.

"Yeah, I see how that can spice things up."

"Right." She stared at her shoes bashfully.

"There's only one thing I don't get."

"What's that?"

"You called me 'strange,'" Mahesh said with a smile.

She smirked. "Yes."

He raised an eyebrow. "In a good or bad way?"

"Different. I'd say you *definitely* are different from other boys I have met in school and college."

"Hmm." He cast her a curious look.

"In a good way, really. In a very good way," Aarvi said softly, smiling.

"Oh, I am relieved to hear that. For a moment, I was worried." Mahesh chuckled.

"I do have a question for you, though," Aarvi said, meeting his eyes.

"What's that?"

"At Hari Uncle's, when he said that even educated women have a raw deal in this country, you agreed."

"Well, they do. I know things are changing—they've certainly changed since the forties and fifties—but not fast enough if you ask me. Don't you agree?"

"Somewhat, yes. I was just wondering what made you say that," Aarvi said.

"I think as a society, we ought to ask ourselves what we are aiming for. If it's to have the most educated housewives in the world, then that's quite a travesty."

"True. On that, I have to agree," Aarvi affirmed. "I was wondering when you made that comment whether you had anyone in mind."

"My mother graduated from Benares Hindu University. That in itself was rare thirty years ago for women. Then my grandparents married her off to my father, and they settled in Calcutta. She never considered having a job or a career. Sure, bringing up four kids was a full-time job, and I suppose she did it happily."

"Maybe that was her choice," Aarvi remarked.

"It was, but that's not my point. She was almost programmed to accept that once she got married. Her only job would be to raise the kids, and my father would take care of earning a living. It's almost as if she was made to feel that she didn't have a choice," Mahesh said.

Aarvi furrowed her brows. "Was she?"

"What do you mean?"

"Was she ever made to feel that she didn't have a choice?" she prodded.

"Not in as many words. But in many subtle ways, societal norms and traditions made her feel—and even worse, accept—that giving up a job and career was the right thing to do," Mahesh insisted.

"Did she ever regret it?"

"I don't know. I only heard her talking about it once, during an argument with my father. Things were not going well financially at the time, and she offered to help by taking up a job. The rest of the family, including my maternal grandparents, flatly refused, and it didn't go any further," Mahesh said.

"It may be a bit presumptuous of you to think what is, or was, right for her. Don't you think?"

"Yes, you are probably right. But, you know, a job is not only for making money. It's doing something that you want, something you like. It's being independent, making a difference, having a say, being confident, and all those other intangibles that are so much more important than money."

"Having a say? You obviously haven't met my family. My mother's the only one who has a say on anything, and the rest of the family has to cater to her needs and demands," Aarvi said, and they both laughed.

They sat together silently for a few more minutes. Aarvi noticed Mahesh staring at the river, gazing at the opposite bank. She knew he was right in many ways. She had never questioned her parents, in-laws, or even Jeev on whether she should continue working at the store after her marriage. It was almost understood that she would move in with Jeev's family and take care of household duties. A job or career for Aarvi had never even been discussed.

They slowly wandered back to the bookstore after finishing their drinks.

"Jeev and his parents are coming over for dinner. I have to leave soon," Aarvi said softly.

"Oh, do you want me to drop you off at home? I can head to Karan's house afterward."

"No, that's fine."

"When will you know whether you can come with me to Jaunpur tomorrow?" Mahesh asked.

"I will know tonight, and I'll call you at the guesthouse and leave a message at the front desk one way or the other. If I am able to go, we can leave from the store around 10:00 a.m."

"Sure. I hope you can make it."

"Me too," Aarvi replied, her mind swimming with thoughts. "Can I ask you a favor?"

"Of course."

"Can I take the book of poems back home with me? I want to read it again tonight."

"Absolutely," Mahesh replied, taking out the notebook carefully and handing it to Aarvi.

"What if Mira is not there? We are going all the way to Jaunpur without really knowing that she is even home."

"I know. I was thinking about that. What else can we do, though? We have to take the chance. It's already Wednesday, and I only have three more days. I think we have to just go and hope that we find her, and that she will meet with us. If not, we can just leave the book in an envelope at her home."

"We could do that. I hope we do see her or else it will feel like a wasted trip," Aarvi said, staring in the direction of the bookstore.

"Not really."

"What do you mean?"

"It wouldn't be a wasted trip for you, even if we don't see Mira," Mahesh asserted, and then smiled.

"Why not?"

"You get to spend the day with me. I can't imagine that would be a waste for anyone."

"Really," Aarvi said with a laugh. "Well, I am happy to admit that I do enjoy your company."

Mahesh bade Aarvi goodbye at the bookstore. "Well, I'm off. Looks like I still have time to go to the guesthouse, freshen up, pick up some barfis and laddoos, and then head to Karan's house for dinner."

"Sounds good. See you tomorrow," Aarvi said, walking into the store.

* * *

When Aarvi and Tarun arrived home, they could already hear Ritika barking orders at the cook and servants to get everything in order before Jeev and his parents arrived. Thinking it best to stay out of the way, Aarvi headed straight to her room, took a quick shower, and freshened up before the guests arrived. Since she had a few extra minutes, she looked through the rest of the sentences from the puzzles.

Should providence take him prematurely, death can help.

Look for death near the Deer Park where the Buddha preached.

Although the details were unclear, the clues that pointed to the Deer Park and Buddha could only be referring to Sarnath. The Deer Park in Sarnath was where Buddha was said to have shared his teachings. *If only I could talk to Mahesh,* Aarvi thought.

She picked up the book of poems and started reading it. Even for someone who was not into poetry, she was moved by some of them. They were not all about romance. Some were about friendship, others were funny, and some referred to events that had happened during Devesh's college days. Halfway through the book, the tone, handwriting, and genre of the poems changed. They shifted to relationships, romance, and love. A few pages farther along, there were a few about loss, then longing, and finally acceptance.

The last few pages featured poems about the wonders of education and the pride that came with teaching a new generation. It was evident that Devesh had loved teaching and had been proud of his students' accomplishments. Aarvi marveled at not only the language and the beautiful words, but also the handwriting in the notebook. She looked for dates associated with the poems but found none. She wondered if the professor had ever considered publishing the collection.

After reading the notebook, Aarvi felt a sense of satisfaction knowing that it would be delivered to the rightful owner. She put it down and debated whether to call Mahesh and tell him all about it. *He must be with Karan,* she thought. While all this was going through her head, she heard the unmistakable shrill of her mother shouting her name to inform her that Jeev and his parents had arrived. She headed downstairs to meet them.

* * *

With only a week and a half to go, the wedding dominated the conversation between Aarvi's and Jeev's parents. Most of the arrangements had been sorted out. The venues for the ceremony, lodging for the guests, caterers for the meals, and entertainment had all been meticulously planned. After spending an hour in the drawing room, everyone moved to the dinner table, and the discussion switched to all the events planned prior to the wedding.

One of them was on Saturday evening, a week before the marriage ceremony, at the Lal home. Jeev and Aarvi had invited some close friends and family for a get-together. Tarun had booked a caterer for the outdoor event and arranged to use the ground floor and garden as the venue for an elaborate dinner. A local band had been hired to entertain the guests in the evening.

As the conversation continued around the dining table, Tarun and Ritika noticed that Aarvi seemed absent-minded. She was polite as always, but not fully engaged in the conversation. Jeev asked Aarvi if anything was bothering her, and she mentioned that she was tired.

Ritika took this to mean she was spending too much time at the bookstore. She started discussing with Jeev's mother how they were both looking forward to Aarvi's married life and how the two should focus on starting a family. When the two mothers were deliberating all this, Tarun noticed that Aarvi's demeanor changed suddenly. She became quiet and subdued. Throughout the rest of the conversation, she had a distant look and would only occasionally smile at them. It was uncharacteristic of Aarvi to not initiate any conversation.

* * *

Once dinner was over, Jeev and Aarvi moved to the drawing room while their parents stayed at the dining table. Aarvi wondered whether Jeev had also noticed that she had been distracted all evening. She was glad that he didn't bring it up. They spent the next half hour going through the guest list for Saturday evening. It had to be increased for some last-minute additions on both sides. Then they spoke about the band and what they should be playing.

Finally, after almost two and a half hours, Jeev and his parents left. Aarvi and her parents were exhausted, though Ritika seemed to have had the best time with Jeev's mother. That didn't stop her from confronting Aarvi.

"What was wrong with you?" Ritika snapped.

"What do you mean?" Aarvi asked, matching her sharp tone. She could see from the corner of her eye that Tarun was getting ready to retreat to his room.

"Don't think they didn't notice that you were not all here during their visit. Your mind was elsewhere, and you were so quiet. Is everything all right?"

"Yes. I am just tired, that's all."

"Well, I am not surprised. Can you stop going to the bookstore? Working and spending time there is not helping," Ritika huffed.

"I like working there," Aarvi responded firmly.

"Well, I am glad that will stop once you are married. In any case, your father also needs to get used to figuring things out on his own at the store. Maybe this will push him to take Ashish there."

"Why?"

"What do you mean?"

"Why do I have to stop working at the store?" Aarvi demanded.

Ritika stared wide-eyed at her, mouth agape. "I don't understand. Once you are married, you will be with Jeev and will have to manage his household."

"So?"

"What do you mean, 'So?' Are you completely out of your mind?"

"Not really," Aarvi blurted, glaring at Ritika.

"I thought it was understood that once you were married, that was going to be the case!" Ritika bellowed in an irritated voice.

"Who decided that? No one asked me," Aarvi continued, crossing her arms.

"I am not dealing with this nonsense! I knew that you working at the store was a bad idea right from the start. Your father insisted on it, and now look what has happened!" Ritika yelled.

"It's not his fault. I wanted to work there. It's the best part of my day, and I enjoy it. I am happy there. What I don't understand is why *you* never bothered to find out why that's the case."

"All right. I am going to my room. I will let your father deal with this. He is the one who put all this in your head, so he should be the one resolving this," Ritika said. She got up, still scowling.

Aarvi was well aware that this was typical of her mother when she knew she couldn't argue anymore. Ritika glowered at her, turned, and left.

Tarun had been watching all this from the comfort of his armchair. He followed his wife into the bedroom while Aarvi trudged back up the stairs to her room and closed the door.

The argument had left her sad, angry, and tired. Her mother was right about one thing: Aarvi had never explicitly expressed a desire to work at the store, or for that matter, to work anywhere after her wedding. That was part of the reason why Ritika, and everyone else, felt that it was understood that Aarvi would not continue working at the store. Nevertheless, Aarvi was angry that no one had actually asked her what she wanted.

She lay down on her bed, exhausted, and closed her eyes. After a few minutes, she turned to pick up the notebook and started rereading some of the poems. Just before she was going to turn off the lights, she heard a knock on the door. Tarun shuffled into the room, looking worried, and sat down on the desk chair.

Aarvi sat up in bed. "Are you worried about Mom?" she asked.

"No, I am worried about you."

"Why?"

"What's going on? I haven't seen you like this. Your mother is right. We all noticed that you weren't yourself this evening. You were defensive while discussing your time at the store, and you drifted in and out of the conversation. Is everything all right?"

"Yes, I am fine," Aarvi responded affectionately. She knew that, despite all his faults, her father genuinely cared about her point of view. Unlike Ritika, Tarun always gave Aarvi a fair hearing. And at times, he would try to smooth things over with her mother, even when he didn't necessarily agree with Aarvi.

"Does it have anything to do with the wedding? Are things all right with Jeev?" Tarun asked.

"Jeev and I are fine."

"Then?"

She paused, staring down at her bedsheets. "I just feel frustrated that I am now expected to be part of Jeev's household and I can't be at the store. You know I really enjoy working there."

"You've never said anything to suggest you would want to continue working there," Tarun claimed.

"Or anywhere," Aarvi blurted.

"What do you mean?"

"I mean, why is it a given that I wouldn't want to work?" Aarvi asked.

A silence fell over Tarun, and Aarvi could see that he was genuinely concerned about her predicament. He looked at her, got up from the chair, and sat down on the bed in front of her.

"Listen. Never mind what your mother says, or anyone else, for that matter. Once you are married, you and Jeev can talk this over and decide what you want to do."

"Why does he get to decide what I want to do?" Aarvi said with an edge to her voice.

"Now, I never said that. I said you must decide together, and that goes for him too. Look at our marriage. Your mother decides everything. We discuss things, but then she makes all the decisions," Tarun said with a smile.

"It's not the same, and you know that."

"I know. But I am sure you can work this out with Jeev," Tarun pleaded.

"What about you? You want Ashish to manage the store, even though he is not interested in it," Aarvi continued.

She could sense that Tarun was mulling things over before responding. She gave him some time to gather his thoughts.

"Well, I honestly never considered the option of having you involved with the store after your wedding.

That's why I was trying to coax your brother into helping me. Of course, it would be good for him too. He is an irresponsible kid. Giving him something to do might actually instill some discipline in him," Tarun said.

"I thought it was because he is the natural heir to your business, and I am not."

"What on earth made you think that?" Tarun asked, straightening his back.

"Mom keeps telling us that Ashish will take over the store and it will be his."

"To run it, yes. But not in terms of inheritance. This might surprise you, but your mom also wants the store to go to both of you after we pass, in equal measure. I know how much the bookstore means to you, and I have never considered leaving it only for Ashish."

Aarvi shrugged. "You never stated otherwise."

"Your mom wanted you, and still wants you, to focus on the wedding. And of course, she wants Ashish to get involved with the store. That's where we differ in our opinion."

"I think that you always cave into Mom's wishes, no matter the issue," scoffed Aarvi.

"That's true, but only up to a point. If there's something that I think is not right when it comes to my kids, I do have my say. Your mom wanted to marry you off after high school, and I insisted that you finish your college degree. She also didn't want you to work at the store, but I managed to convince her that it's a good idea, something that makes you happy. She never wanted you to go on school and college trips outside the city, but I stepped in, knowing that it was something that would do you good."

"That's true," Aarvi said, scooting closer to her father. The affectionate tone in her father's voice calmed her down.

"Not every argument or decision needs to be settled with a raised voice. Sometimes it's best to wait until folks are calm and then work it out."

"How come we don't see this side of you at the bookstore?"

Tarun laughed, placing an affectionate hand on his daughter's forehead. Aarvi embraced him and then pulled back to look him in the eye. "There are two other things I want to talk to you about," she murmured.

"What are they?"

"I am going to Jaunpur tomorrow," Aarvi announced.

"Why? Is it to meet that supplier? I thought everything was sorted out over the phone. If not, I can send someone else."

"No. It has to do with what Devesh Uncle had left us."

"Ah, those puzzles."

She nodded meekly and murmured, "That's right."

"So, you are going with Mahesh?"

"Yes," Aarvi replied, wondering whether her father's demeanor would change upon hearing this.

It didn't. Instead, he was curious. "We never really talked about what's going on with those puzzles and papers that Devesh left you."

"I don't want to talk about it now. But I will tell you everything once we have solved it all."

"You are not putting yourself in any danger, right? Should I be worried?"

"No, but it's important for me to get to the truth," Aarvi responded.

He paused for a moment, stroking his chin. "How will you go? Shall I arrange a car and a driver to take you and Mahesh there?"

"Mahesh is asking his friend whether he can take his car. If not, then we can book one tomorrow."

"Yes, it shouldn't be a problem getting a car for the day. Jaunpur is almost four hours away. I am guessing you are not visiting too many places."

"We are not, and it shouldn't take that long in Jaunpur. We will be back by evening," Aarvi said.

She could see that he was apprehensive as he looked away. Then he turned back to her and smiled. "All right. If this is important enough that you think you need to go, that's fine."

"Thank you," Aarvi said, hugging her father again.

After another moment, he looked at her. "What's the other thing?" Tarun asked.

"What?"

"You said you wanted to talk about two things."

"Ah yes. I want to invite Mahesh and his friend Karan to our dinner this Saturday. We are adding guests, and now the number of people coming has ballooned to nearly sixty. Two more shouldn't make a difference," Aarvi said in a hurry. She locked eyes with him to see if his expression would change after this request. It didn't.

"It won't. It should be fine," Tarun said and got up. He kissed her on her forehead before walking to the door. Turning around, he took one last look at Aarvi, who was smiling and feeling much better. She knew from his expression that he was pleased as well.

"Thank you," Aarvi said, still smiling.

"Let me deal with the Jaunpur trip with your mother."

"Sure," Aarvi said, feeling a flood of relief.

"Mahesh is a good boy," Tarun said.

Before he could continue, Aarvi said, grinning, "I know that. I have spent some time with him this week. How do *you* know that?" she asked.

"Oh, I don't know him at all. I just know that my daughter wouldn't spend so much time with anyone unless he is good, and she really likes him," Tarun said with an affectionate smile before leaving the room.

* * *

Mahesh had just finished dinner with Karan and his family. The lively feast had lasted almost two hours, leaving Mahesh exhausted. Karan's family was large, loud, opinionated, and generous. They all had an opinion on Mahesh's decision to go abroad. There was an argument between Karan's father and uncle on one side and Karan's cousins on the other, as to why youngsters like Mahesh were leaving India. Finally, when they had all eaten and argued enough, they showered their wishes and blessings on Mahesh and left. He sensed that Karan was happy to see the back of most of them and was looking forward to some time alone with his friend.

Mahesh made a quick call to the guesthouse to let them know that if Aarvi called, they could inform her that they would be going to Jaunpur the next day in Karan's car. Then Karan and Mahesh moved out of the house to the sprawling garden that held some chairs and sofas.

Karan asked a servant for some tea, and they settled into a couple of armchairs in front of the house. From this vantage point, the entire facade of the big, three-story house was visible. On the other side, they could see the entire property up to the gates. Karan's was a large, joint family. While these types of units were slowly disappearing with more nuclear families on the rise, old business families still maintained big houses with joint ownership and habitation. With each passing generation, such establishments were becoming rarer.

The younger generation also wanted more freedom and privacy, and if they could afford it, they moved out. This meant Karan's lifestyle was gradually becoming the exception. Mahesh could sense the tension between Karan and his wife, Suneeta, during the evening. It was evident that Suneeta came from a modern, less conservative family and was trying her level best to convince Karan that moving out would be the best thing for their relationship. Unlike the other women in Karan's family, Suneeta was in the workforce. Karan had told Mahesh that this was a compromise he had gotten the rest of the family to agree to. But the arguments to reach that compromise had left some tension between him and his father.

Once the tea arrived, Mahesh and Karan sat side by side looking into the starry night.

"Thanks for the car, by the way. Not just for tomorrow, but the entire week."

"Oh, come off it. It's the least I could do. I wish I could come with you to Jaunpur tomorrow. It would be a break from my hectic, day-to-day routine," Karan said with a sigh.

"All good?"

"Yes, but staying in a joint family has its ups and downs."

"How are things with Suneeta? Is she still upset?" Mahesh asked gently.

"We have our moments. I am always caught in a tug-of-war, struggling to keep her and the rest of the family happy. Trust me, if I could move out, I would."

"Well, she is a fine girl. You know, when we came to your wedding, we actually discussed that."

"What exactly?" Karan asked, slightly amused.

"How did you rope in a girl like Suneeta? I mean, honestly, whatever did she see in you?"

"You mean apart from my good looks, right?" Karan said, and they both broke into fits of laughter.

They spoke for a few minutes about their days in Delhi, and then the conversation switched back to Devesh.

"Did you find out more about the professor's family?" Mahesh asked.

"I did. Not specifically about the family, but about Laxman."

"What about him?"

"Laxman's business is not doing so well. It seems he has taken on a lot of debt," Karan said.

"His real estate business?"

"Yes. It seems his latest venture failed miserably, and he still owes a lot of money to the banks and some private investors."

Mahesh leaned forward in his chair. "So, he's in trouble financially?"

"So it would seem."

"Do you know when it all started?"

"It's hard to say. But I found out that he did come about a year ago asking my father to invest in one of the properties he was developing," Karan added.

"Around the time that the professor had his accident?"

Karan changed his posture, sitting upright. "What exactly are you suggesting?"

"I am not suggesting anything. I am just looking at the clues that the professor left us. If indeed Laxman was involved in some foul play concerning his uncle's accident and death, then what you just said gives him motive."

"True, although it could be just that—an accident," Karan insisted.

"I'd have thought the same had it not been for the clues and what the professor's loyal servant told us." Mahesh then told Karan about his conversation with Kulwant at the yoga club.

With a pensive expression, Karan said, "The accident was reported to the authorities, you know, as is usually the case for hit-and-runs. It was investigated by the police, and they couldn't locate the lorry or the driver. The driver didn't stop, and there were no witnesses. I know this because the fellow who investigated the incident was one of the professor's ex-students from Delhi University." He sipped his tea.

Mahesh leaned forward until he was on the edge of his chair. "Who is that?"

"Bhanu Dev, a police officer from the Sarnath Police Station. The professor's residence falls under that station's jurisdiction. Before you ask, he is a senior fellow, not from our batch. He graduated well before we went to college."

Mahesh sat back, the wheels in his mind turning. "Does Laxman's company own any lorries?"

"Of course they do. They are in real estate and construction. It's not uncommon for these companies to own several trucks. But so do many other companies."

"Hmm." He rubbed his chin in thought.

"So, what's the deal with Jaunpur?" Karan asked.

"Ah, I was wondering when you would ask about that." Mahesh recounted to Karan how they had found the book of poems and the reason for their trip.

"Wow. The professor was a colorful fellow, it seems," Karan said.

"Yes. Well, we're hoping to find out more tomorrow. College romances aren't uncommon in any decade. I know we are talking about the late forties or early fifties. Still, I'm not sure what's so surprising or scandalous about it all."

"True. Say, did you ask your new friend Aarvi about what we discussed earlier?" Karan asked, switching topics.

"What's that?"

"Why did the professor select the two of you?"

Mahesh shook his head. "No, we didn't discuss that. It's quite clear why he chose us."

"Why?"

A Poet's Ballad, A Crossword Mystery

"We are both into solving crossword puzzles. He had to leave clues for quick-thinking, intelligent people who could solve them. He couldn't have possibly wasted his time in leaving them for lesser mortals," Mahesh said with a playful smile.

"Really?" Karan laughed.

"You still think he selected me and Aarvi for some other reason?"

"It has to be. What you said about the puzzles makes sense, but I think there is more to it than that," Karan insisted.

"But what?" Mahesh sat back, pondering his point.

"I don't know," Karan started and then added jovially, "Maybe he thought you and Aarvi would be a great match. Perhaps he thought that the two of you would fall hopelessly in love. You would give up on London, and she would break her engagement and run off with you to some obscure Indian town. Then you'd get married and live unhappily ever after."

"Unbelievable how your mind works," Mahesh said, chuckling.

"Yes, I know. I surprise myself sometimes," Karan said and smiled. "Well, I must say she is a nice girl."

"How do you know?" Mahesh asked, knowing full well that another snide remark was on its way.

"Oh, I don't know her. But I know you. Putting up with you every day for hours takes some patience and character. I don't know how anyone could do it unless they were really, *really* nice," Karan replied with a boisterous laugh.

Mahesh rolled his eyes. "Well, I will be sure to let her know what you think."

As it approached midnight, Mahesh thanked Karan and then headed back to the guesthouse. On the way back, he mentally replayed the conversation around Devesh's accident and death in light of what he had just learned from Karan. His friend had unknowingly helped him solve the next two lines of the puzzle.

* * *

Mahesh lingered in front of the Sanskriti Bookshop, waiting for Aarvi. He had picked a spot beneath a large tree facing the store, sitting down on a wooden bench meant for tourists. He then started sifting through all the papers in Devesh's file. The store was open, and he could have waited inside, but the skies were overcast, and a cool breeze made the morning more pleasant.

Things were quiet outside the store this Thursday morning, which reminded Mahesh that he only had two more days in Benares. A week from Saturday, he would be on his way to London.

He closed the file and started thinking about the following week when his parents would come to Delhi to see him off. They had already booked a small hotel, and he would take them around the city while they were visiting. He knew that his parents, especially his mother, were sad to see him leave. His father was busy running the family business, which occupied most of his time. His mother also kept busy with an active social circle, not to mention his siblings and their families. But Mahesh knew that being the youngest, he was always more special, or at least his mother made him feel that way.

Then his thoughts shifted to his time in Benares. Although he was spending most of his time trying to figure out what Devesh had left for him, what he would remember most from this trip was Aarvi. She had made it enjoyable and memorable. While his mind was wandering, he felt a gentle tap on his right shoulder.

"Lost in thought, are we?" Aarvi said with a teasing smile.

"Yes, we historians tend to do that," Mahesh responded, beaming at the sight of her.

"You could have waited inside the store, you know."

"Oh, that's all right. I was just enjoying the sights and sounds of your wonderful city."

"Anything interesting?"

"Yes. I always knew Benares had a lot to offer, but this time around, I am very impressed with the people. Especially my partner in crime," Mahesh pronounced.

"Ha!" Aarvi replied, her smile widening. "Sorry it took so long. My mother insisted that I put henna on my hands before leaving in preparation for a pre-wedding puja at our house." She showed him her hands, which bore a beautiful, decorative design of a lotus imprinted on her palms when she brought them together, giving the impression that they were connected.

"Wow, they look so beautiful," Mahesh remarked, looking at her palms and then at her.

"Thank you."

He gathered up his papers and documents. "So, all good for our trip to Jaunpur?"

"Yes, all sorted out."

"Wonderful," Mahesh said as they walked to the car parked a few steps away.

Soon they were on their way. Getting out of the city took a while due to the narrow lanes and crowded streets. Once the car headed north toward the highway, it slowly picked up speed. They rolled down their windows. The breeze made them feel comfortable despite the summer sun. Aarvi pointed out all the landmarks they crossed. She even showed Mahesh the school she had attended when they drove past it.

Once on the highway, Mahesh shared Karan's revelations about Laxman's business, his financial troubles, and the police probe into Devesh's accident. They spent the next hour discussing everything they had learned so far, occasionally taking breaks to look out the window, marveling at the countryside.

A little over two hours into their journey, the driver informed them that they were halfway to Jaunpur. They decided to take a break at a small roadside dhaba. Getting out to stretch their legs, they bought some soft drinks, and Mahesh shared the sandwiches that he had packed. While sitting across from each other at the dhaba on wooden stools, Mahesh told Aarvi more about Karan.

"By the way, he thinks we are missing something," Mahesh said, taking a last big bite out of his sandwich.

"Missing? Like what?" Aarvi had polished off her meal and was now enjoying her cold Fanta.

"Why he chose us. You know, for all these puzzles and clues."

"That's exactly *why* he chose us," Aarvi affirmed.

"That's what I think and what I told Karan. After all, he had to select intelligent, good-looking people to solve all this."

"Oh, really?" She crossed her arms playfully.

He nodded decidedly.

"Well, I can't really disagree with that, you know," Aarvi said, and they both laughed.

"There's one thing, though. He did take quite a gamble on us. I mean, we could have easily disregarded all of this. It was just by chance that I came to Benares to pick up what he left for me. He couldn't have possibly known that we would meet and try to figure this out together."

"That's true. All this could just have easily not happened."

Mahesh met her eyes. "Well, I am glad it did. Otherwise, I wouldn't have met you."

"True," Aarvi said, averting her gaze.

It suddenly dawned on Mahesh that he would be leaving in three days, and most likely, he would never see her again. He wondered if Aarvi felt the same way.

He cleared his throat, changing the subject. "And this thing with the college romance and the book of poems. College romances aren't uncommon, although writing poetry probably is. How are they?"

"What?" Aarvi cocked her head.

"The poems? You read them again—did we miss anything? Were they better when you reread them?"

"Ah yes. I enjoyed reading them again, and no, I don't think I chanced upon any new clues," Aarvi replied, finishing off her soda. "So, how common was it for you?"

"What?"

"College romances? You were in Delhi, no parents nearby, a university full of boys and girls," Aarvi said with a smile.

"Right," Mahesh said. "Sadly, nothing much to report. I did go on dates, and obviously, I have friends from university who are girls. But nothing serious."

"Oh, I am surprised."

"Why?" Mahesh asked, holding back a smile.

"I don't know. You seem all right. Sure, I've only known you for a few days. But you are pleasant company, and I think you are worth a shot," Aarvi said with a mischievous sparkle in her eye.

"Thank you. That's exactly the kind of endorsement I needed for my confidence," Mahesh said.

Just then, they noticed the driver, who was enjoying a cup of tea farther out, walking toward them. That was their cue to head to the car and resume their journey. As they continued their road trip, they spoke about their days in college and their interests.

"Why history?" Aarvi turned sideways to look at Mahesh.

"Interest, I suppose. History changes with time, you know. Over time, people learn new things about past events. Usually, history is written by rulers of the era or narrated by people who are influenced by them. So, it comes with its own set of biases. Slowly, as new anecdotes and things emerge, we start seeing the past through a different lens. I find that fascinating."

Aarvi sighed. "It's unfortunate the way the subject is taught in our schools and colleges. There's too much emphasis on dates and events. It takes the joy out of learning."

"That's true."

"In a country where everyone is racing to be engineers, lawyers, or doctors, pursuing history as a degree and career is rather strange."

"Yes, I have heard that. But I really didn't like those other subjects. I think we ought to have more varied choices."

"How so?" Aarvi asked.

Mahesh paused for a few seconds before responding. "Well, there's no reason why someone who likes history and geography shouldn't also be able to take courses in, let's say, astronomy or architecture."

"True. I have often wondered why they restrict things in our colleges and force us to pick subjects only in our area. I am guessing it's not as restrictive abroad."

"Depends on the university and program, but in general, you are right. There are more options abroad."

"Is that what you are planning to do—broaden your horizons?"

"Yes, well, in a PhD program, you do need to focus on a specific area. But you are right. I am planning on taking courses in archeology and philosophy to see where that leads."

"You are not sure what you will do afterward?"

"No, I haven't figured it out yet."

"Hmm." Aarvi's expression took on a thoughtful look.

"You find that a bit odd, don't you?" Mahesh asked.

"Yes. Most people seem to have things figured out, like what they want to study, where they want to work, when they would like to get married, and so on."

"True. I guess I am not one of them."

"Do you plan on staying abroad after you graduate?" Aarvi asked, fiddling with her handkerchief.

"I don't know," Mahesh said, shaking his head and sighing. "Honestly, I think I will just see how things go."

"Are you worried about what you will do afterward?"

"Yes, I am a bit scared. But I also know that if I don't seize this opportunity, I will regret it later and wonder what would have happened."

"I guess that makes some sense. But you will be there for a while, right? From what I've heard, a PhD takes five years, doesn't it?"

"Typically, yes," Mahesh confirmed.

Aarvi gave him a knowing look. "It's hard to come back after that. I don't think there are too many opportunities here other than teaching."

"That's true. One of my friends in Delhi said the same thing."

"That said, I'm not sure there are many people who can do what you're doing."

"Well, I really don't feel like much of a trailblazer. I agree it's more common to go abroad for science and technical degrees. But I think things are changing. Anyway, how about you? Are you all set for your wedding next Saturday?"

"Yes," Aarvi mumbled, looking away.

Mahesh wondered why she always averted her gaze and became quiet when the topic switched to her marriage. No matter how hard he tried, he couldn't decipher her stoic expression.

As the conversation faded, they both looked out the window. They were passing through a small town, still about an hour away from Jaunpur.

"Do you want to eat something before seeing Mira?" Mahesh asked.

"I can wait till after the visit, if that's fine with you."

"Sure. I am hoping we do get to meet her and give her the notebook."

"Me too. Maybe we'll get some answers about Devesh Uncle as well."

They spent the next hour gazing out the window and occasionally chatting about Indian politics, cricket, and Bollywood. When they reached the neighborhood where the address was located, the driver got out to ask a shopkeeper for directions. A few minutes later, they stopped in front of an apartment building in a large housing colony.

Mahesh asked the driver to park the car out front, and they made their way to the second floor and knocked on the door. It was opened by an older gentleman who looked like either a cook or help. They asked him if they could meet Mira Kapoor and then waited outside while he slipped back in.

A moment later, a lady dressed impeccably in a bright-yellow saree appeared and introduced herself to Mahesh and Aarvi. Despite her graying hair, she had a youthful look and a pleasing disposition.

"My name is Mahesh, and this is Aarvi. We are here to give you something from Professor Devesh Tripathi. He passed away a few weeks ago," Mahesh said, glancing at Aarvi, who smiled and nodded.

"Oh, I am so sorry to hear that. Please, come inside," Mira said.

She led them into a large drawing room and asked them to sit on a sofa near a window. The room was well lit with some armchairs across from the sofa and a coffee table in between. Some walls were lined with shelves teeming with books, photographs, and souvenirs. Other walls were filled with paintings and more photographs. At the far end of the room was a dining table and, behind it, a large door leading to the rest of the apartment. It was evident that the room had been decorated meticulously.

A Poet's Ballad, A Crossword Mystery

They sat down, and Mira called for her cook and asked him to bring some refreshments. After exchanging a few pleasantries, Aarvi brought out Devesh's notebook.

"Mahesh and I knew the professor, although I can't say that we were very close to him," Aarvi said. Mahesh noticed Mira peering at the notebook on the coffee table.

"Is this what you are here about?" Mira asked, looking at Aarvi.

"Yes."

"And he left this with you for me?"

"Not quite," Aarvi replied. Then Mahesh and Aarvi took turns explaining how Devesh had left crossword puzzles and how they had solved them.

"Wow, that's interesting indeed," Mira said, her wide-eyed expression hinting that she was still trying to absorb it all. Mahesh and Aarvi were careful not to tell her about the clues pointing to Devesh's accident and death.

"If you don't mind, ma'am, how did you know Devesh? The only thing we could gather was that you were friends and were close in university," Mahesh said, hoping to learn more.

"Yes, that's right. We were very close during our college days in Benares. Then life took us in different directions. I moved back here to Jaunpur, and from what I know, he left for Delhi. I didn't keep in touch with him afterward. Occasionally, I would hear something from our mutual acquaintances," Mira said. She then started reminiscing about her days in college. It was evident from her commentary that she had enjoyed her time at Benares Hindu University and that she and Devesh had been very close. Mahesh could sense that Mira didn't want to elaborate on why her relationship with Devesh ended, so he chose not to press further. She told them that after returning to Jaunpur, she got married and had a daughter. Mira's husband was a retired government employee; he was currently out on an errand.

After a few minutes, the cook arrived with some gulab jamuns, jalebis, and tea, and placed them on the coffee table beside Devesh's notebook.

"Thank you, ma'am, for the sweets and tea. You really didn't have to," Aarvi said.

"Oh no. Not at all. You come bearing a gift from a very special friend from another time. I really appreciate it," Mira said, getting up to serve the sweets to them on small plates.

They spent the next few minutes eating and sipping their tea. Meanwhile, Mira picked up the notebook and slowly leafed through it. She stopped every now and then, read a passage, and smiled.

"Did the professor ever tell you that he wrote poetry?" Mahesh asked.

"Oh yes. Devesh wrote lots of things in college. Most of it, at least I thought, was funny. But I can see that over the years, he wrote about a whole range of emotions. These are quite sentimental and very personal."

"Yes," Aarvi agreed.

"So, you have read them?" Mira asked, glancing between Aarvi and Mahesh.

"We have. I hope you don't mind," Aarvi responded.

"Oh, not at all. What do you think about them, Aarvi?"

"I think they are very good. I am not sure why he never got them published."

"Because he wrote them for himself," Mira said and then suddenly became quiet.

"And he left them for you," Aarvi added softly.

She wasn't sure whether Mira heard her comment. After a minute or so, Mira looked up. "Yes, that he did. What am I supposed to do with it?"

"We are not sure, ma'am. We only wanted to leave it with the rightful owner," Aarvi said as she picked up her cup to take a sip of tea.

"Thank you. I do appreciate that," Mira said as she got up. "Oh, let me get you some water. Give me a minute." Before Aarvi and Mahesh could say anything, she had disappeared into the other room.

Mahesh left the couch to look at the photographs on the bookshelves. There were so many of them. The photos were mostly of Mira, her husband, and her daughter. A few others, he assumed, were either extended family or friends. Aarvi was still seated on the sofa, studying the room from her vantage point.

Mahesh stopped suddenly in front of a photograph, staring at it intently. He turned around and locked eyes with Aarvi. He didn't have to say anything. Aarvi quickly got up and walked over to see what Mahesh was pointing to.

It was a close-up portrait of Mira's daughter. She was a spitting image of Devesh—it was impossible not to see the resemblance. She had the same eyes, hair, and smile. The most noticeable resemblance was the cleft on her chin, which was identical to Devesh's.

"So that was the scandal," Mahesh murmured.

"Yes," whispered Aarvi. "She became pregnant. That's why she left in a hurry during the final year of college and why her parents married her off quickly."

"Probably. We don't know for sure, but I think you may be right."

"We can't possibly ask her unless she tells us herself," Aarvi uttered, taking darting glances at the door to make sure they were alone.

"Right," Mahesh said quickly. They heard footsteps from the other room, and they scurried back to the sofa, sitting upright.

Within a few seconds, Mira returned with a tray of two water glasses and placed them on the coffee table. "Are you going back to Benares today?" she asked.

"Yes," Aarvi and Mahesh replied hurriedly. He wondered whether Mira noticed their sudden change of tone. It was louder and more guarded.

"You really came all the way just to give me Devesh's notebook?"

"We did," Aarvi replied.

"That's so kind of you."

"You have nice photographs," Mahesh said politely, pointing to the shelf where her daughter's photograph stood.

"Oh yes. They are mostly of my husband and our daughter. She lives in Bombay now with her husband. They are expecting their first child in a few weeks."

"That's exciting," Mahesh replied. "Congratulations."

"Thank you. Yes, it's exciting. My daughter is a little older than you and has been married for a while. We are happy that she is starting a family. I see that you have henna on your hands, Aarvi. Is that for a wedding?"

"Yes. I am getting married next Saturday."

"Oh, that's wonderful. Congratulations!" Mira said, looking at them.

"Oh, *w-w-we* are n-n-not getting m-m-married," Aarvi stammered, sounding flustered. "Mahesh is over from Delhi because of what the professor left for him and will be heading back on Sunday. He is going abroad next weekend for further studies."

"That's nice. I am sorry, I just assumed that you were together."

"That's all right," Mahesh responded, casting a glance at Aarvi, who looked slightly embarrassed. He went on to tell Mira about what he was pursuing, and they spent the next few minutes talking about his plans. After almost an hour, they had exhausted what they had planned to talk about. Mira thanked them again for the notebook, her glistening eyes revealing that she was genuinely sad that Devesh had passed.

"We were quite something in college, you know. Actually, I may have an old picture in an album here. Let me show you that before you leave. It may sound strange, but we were young at one time too," Mira said with a smile.

She got up and opened a cabinet. After paging through some papers, she brought out an envelope and started sifting through some photos. From the sofa, Aarvi and Mahesh could see they were old, black-and-white photographs. She narrowed them down to one, held it up, and smiled.

"Here's a good one," she said, turning to Aarvi and Mahesh. She handed it over to them.

Aarvi looked at it first, and Mahesh saw the shock in her expression. Her face froze, and she clutched the photograph tightly, almost bending it. It almost seemed as if she didn't want to hand the picture to Mahesh. Finally, he eased the photograph away from Aarvi and looked at it.

A young Mira and Devesh were sitting on a wooden bench. They seemed happy and very much in love. Then his eyes shifted to a second couple in the photograph. They had an identical pose, smiling, holding hands affectionately. Mahesh quickly realized why Aarvi's expression had changed.

Before he could ask anything, Aarvi spoke up. "This photograph," she said, looking at Mira. She started tapping her feet vigorously on the carpeted floor.

"It's one of the best ones I have of Devesh and me. You can make out it's us, right?"

"Yes, it's a nice picture. There's another couple in it too," Aarvi noted, her eyes glaring at the photograph in Mahesh's hand.

"Oh yes. We were the talk of the town at the time, or at least in the university. It was always going to be me and Devesh, and Tanu and Chitra. Then, as I said, life took us in different directions."

"Tanu?" Aarvi asked.

"Tarun, that was his name, but we called him Tanu. He was with us during college. He is from Benares. I think his family owns a bookstore there," Mira said.

Mahesh handed the photograph back to her and studied the stunned expression on Aarvi's face. Mira took another long look at it, smiled, and gently placed it back in the pile.

Aarvi and Mahesh looked at each other. It was time for them to leave. They thanked Mira again for her hospitality, and she wished them well for their future.

Aarvi and Mahesh slowly walked down the stairs and headed back to where the car was parked. Before reaching the parking lot, they stopped near a roadside stall.

"Well, that was something," Aarvi said, still reeling from seeing her father in the photograph.

"Yes," Mahesh said softly.

"In case you are wondering, my mother's name is not Chitra," Aarvi said. "You know, I could never imagine my father having had a college romance with anyone."

"Karan was right," Mahesh said, locking eyes with Aarvi.

"About what?"

"About the professor selecting us for more than just our ability to solve crosswords," Mahesh said, his voice wavering slightly.

"Did you hear a word I said?" Aarvi demanded.

Mahesh let a silence hang over them for a minute. "Yes—" he started. Before he could continue, Aarvi cut in.

"I am a bit shocked to see my father's picture from his college days, and of course, to learn of his romance. I really know very little about his life back then. He rarely talks about his time in college," Aarvi said as they meandered toward the car. "Sorry, Mahesh. You were saying something when I interrupted you."

"I was going to say that I *was* paying attention to what you were saying. I know your mother isn't Chitra, the woman in the picture with your father." He fixed Aarvi with his gaze. "Chitra is *my* mother."

Kismet

———◈———

The drive back to Benares seemed to fly by. Much of the conversation centered on Mira, her daughter, and what they had uncovered about Tarun and Chitra.

"It doesn't seem right that Devesh Uncle didn't know he had a daughter," Aarvi said, staring out the window as thoughts of him and his family swam in her mind.

"I wonder if things would have been different had he known. I can understand why that was the case," Mahesh murmured.

Aarvi turned to face him and acquiesced by slightly nodding. "Has your mother ever talked to you about her college days?" she asked.

"Yes, but we never talked about her friends. The conversation centered mainly on the fun they had during their college days and how things were different compared with now."

"Nothing specific about any particular friends?"

"No," Mahesh said with a smile. "I don't think parents, in general, want to talk to their children about past relationships."

"True. I have always heard my father speak fondly about his college days, but not about those sorts of things."

"When I came to the bookshop on the first day, your father did tell me that I reminded him of someone. Do you recall?"

"Do you think he knows anything?" Aarvi asked, drumming her fingers on her lap.

Mahesh shook his head. "I doubt it."

"Are you going to speak to your mother about this?" Aarvi continued.

"Oh yes. I will certainly talk to her about my trip to Benares, what we uncovered about the professor, her old friend Tarun, and his marvelous daughter, Aarvi."

"Oh, I am sure she will have so many questions," she said with a sly smile.

"That she will. What about you? Are you going to share this with your father?"

"I am not sure," Aarvi said, eyes downcast. "I don't know what I will do."

"It's not that complicated, you know. Romances happen during college days, and then people move on."

"Yes, but not for everyone. It didn't happen for you and me, for example. Why is that?"

"Right. It doesn't happen for everyone," Mahesh said.

"Any theories as to why it didn't happen for you? Is it just that you didn't meet the right person? Is there even such a thing?" Aarvi asked.

"I don't know whether there is a right person or not. I guess when it happens, it probably seems right. You know, it's not a crime to fall in love."

"Still, that doesn't answer the question of why you didn't find anyone."

He leaned back in the seat, brows scrunched in thought. "I can't say for sure. I guess I found it easier to be around books and play chess. That took a lot of my time. Maybe I just haven't found that connection yet. How about you?"

"I don't know. I wasn't really interested in anyone. Now I am getting married. I have known Jeev and his family for a long time, and I think I always knew I'd end up with him. Maybe that was always in the back of my head," Aarvi noted.

"Well, he is certainly lucky, and I am sure you will make a grand couple."

"Thank you," Aarvi said, again glancing away as conflicting feelings tugged at her heart.

They spent the next few minutes in silence, looking out the window on either side. The late-afternoon sun was still bright on the horizon, and the farmers farther afield were tending their crops. When Aarvi turned to Mahesh, she saw that he had dozed off, his head resting against the window. This way, she could catch a glimpse of his face without him knowing that she was looking at him. She couldn't help but think how different he was from the boys she had met in college and her fiancé. Jeev was closer to her in temperament and outlook, and they came from similar families and backgrounds. There was some comfort in the familiarities and common outlooks.

Yet to Aarvi, there was something strangely appealing in the differences and diverging views that Mahesh held. They forced her to think differently and challenged her to question long-held beliefs and traditions. She didn't know whether that was due to her upcoming marriage, Mahesh, or both. She smiled as she took in Mahesh's resting face.

Suddenly, the car hit a small bump that woke him up, and she quickly looked toward the driver to see if everything was all right. She wasn't sure if Mahesh had caught her staring at him. The driver informed them that it was just a small brick that had startled them.

The car moved at a fair pace, and halfway back to Benares, they stopped at a roadside dhaba for snacks and some tea. Sitting on the rickety benches of a picnic table near the makeshift food stall, they dug into their sweet rajbhogs.

"You fell asleep," Aarvi said between bites. "I didn't think I was such boring company," she added with a mischievous smile.

"Oh, I am so sorry I dozed off. I guess I'm tired. No reflection on you, honestly."

"It's all right. I'm just teasing you." She took another sip of tea. "I was wondering where this leaves us regarding the clues and Devesh Uncle."

"Well, we did hand over the book to Mira, which is what the professor wanted. The next two clues point to the police station in Sarnath and, I believe, Officer Bhanu Dev. I think we ought to pay him a visit."

"Sarnath, I understand. That was in the clues. But Bhanu Dev? How did you deduce that?"

"Actually, it was the other way around. Karan told me that Bhanu Dev is an officer at the Sarnath Police Station. Bhanu is the name of Lord Shiva, the destroyer or lord of death."

"Yes! Of course. 'Should providence take him prematurely, death can help,'" Aarvi pronounced.

"Also, there is a connection between the professor and Bhanu Dev. Bhanu is a former student of his," Mahesh revealed. "That's what Karan told me."

"Well, that should wrap up the mysteries from the puzzles. But then there are the newspaper cuttings," Aarvi remarked, curious whether Mahesh had deciphered the meaning of the other items.

"I was wondering when you would ask me about them and whether you had caught on to their meaning."

"I want to hear what you think first."

"The newspaper cuttings in my box don't seem to have a common thread in terms of subject. Some are movie reviews; others are sports columns. There are also a couple of articles on theaters and one about a school. There is nothing highlighted or marked on any of them," Mahesh commented.

"Understood, so why did he leave them for us?" Aarvi asked, looking Mahesh in the eye.

"The only common thread I could find is who wrote them. They were all written by the same person, Deepika Roy."

"Same here. Everything he left in my folder was written by her as well," Aarvi confirmed.

"I can only assume the professor wanted us to go meet her and have the press, in addition to the police, investigate his death," Mahesh suggested.

"That's what I think too," Aarvi said, finishing off her rajbhog. "It's not a great paper, you know."

"What do you mean?"

"The paper that Deepika Roy works for. It's *The Benares Examiner*. It's a struggling publication with a small circulation even by local standards," Aarvi conveyed.

"I think, from everything we've learned about the clues and the professor, it's more about the person. He is pointing us to specific people. So, our next visits have to be to Bhanu at the Sarnath Police Station and Deepika at *The Benares Examiner*."

"Yes," Aarvi said softly, a sigh escaping her lips.

"Everything all right?"

"Yeah. I guess we just don't have much time."

"You're right. It has to be either tomorrow or Saturday," Mahesh replied. Aarvi felt forlorn knowing they only had two more days together in Benares.

"There is something I have been meaning to ask you," Aarvi said, her tone soft and serious as she met Mahesh's gaze.

"What is it?"

"We are having a function this Saturday evening at our house for close family and friends. It's a small celebration with a band, music, food, and stuff."

"That sounds nice."

"I would like you and Karan to come over."

"Are you sure? I mean, we don't really fall into the close friends and family category. Plus, we won't know many people," Mahesh reasoned.

"Well, both of you will come as my new friends, and that's that."

His face lit up. "How can I possibly refuse? Sure, Aarvi. We will be there. I will ask Karan tonight to see if he can make it."

"Good," Aarvi said, satisfied with Mahesh's response.

"Thank you for inviting us."

A Poet's Ballad, A Crossword Mystery

They returned to the car and were soon on their way back to Benares. The snacks and tea had left them reinvigorated, and they spoke the rest of the way about Devesh, what they had learned, and crossword puzzles.

After a couple of hours, the car reached the outskirts of the city. They came to a standstill near a railway crossing behind a long line of cars, trucks, and buses waiting for the train to pass. In front of their Ambassador was a bus full of young foreigners and backpackers heading into the city. Aarvi pointed toward the vehicle and turned to Mahesh.

"I never understood why people are fascinated with Benares. I can understand that it's one of the holiest cities for Hindus, and pilgrims from all over come to the city for its temples and the Ganges. But these backpackers and tourists from other countries—I'd imagine there are so many other places in India that would be much more interesting and exotic for them."

"Well, they don't always come for the same reason. I mean, anyone can come to visit. Nothing wrong with that. It is a popular destination not just for the temples and the Ganges, but for the place itself," he said.

"So, tell me something, since you are a student of history. We tout ourselves as the oldest living city in India. Is that true? Or is it mainly sentimental thinking?" Aarvi asked, peering at him.

"There is some truth to that. Benares is one of the oldest cities in India, though it is debatable whether it is *the* oldest. We all know that the Indus Valley Civilization predates most of the country's cities, if not all. But most of those places have been destroyed. There are other cities, of course, that are pretty old. It's hard to always put a date on a place. India is an old civilization. I am sure, with time, we will learn new things. Now, if you went by what Mark Twain said, Benares is older than history, older than tradition, older even than legend, and looks twice as old as all of them put together. That, I think, is sentimental and is born from his love for the place," Mahesh said with a smile.

"I have heard that quote from Mark Twain many times," Aarvi said. "My father relishes announcing that to all who lend him an ear."

Mahesh laughed. "Regardless, I don't think folks love Benares just because it's old. I think something about it enchants many of them, and that makes them come back."

"It's hard to see what the young backpackers like about it," she said, glancing at the bus in front.

"The city is different from what they're used to and is charming in other ways, I suppose."

Aarvi shook her head incredulously. "I could never imagine doing something like that."

"Like what?"

"Leaving everything to go backpacking with friends in a different country."

Mahesh shrugged. "People like different things."

"Or going off to study abroad, with no plans for the future, not knowing what will happen after, no plans for marriage, away from your family." Aarvi raised her eyebrows.

"You're talking about me now," Mahesh said.

"I am. I think it would have been easier and more comfortable if you had stayed back, gotten married, and settled down."

"Comfortable, perhaps. Maybe I didn't want that right now."

"Doesn't it bother you that you don't know what you're going to do, where you are going to end up?" Aarvi posed.

"It does cross my mind, yes. As I said before, part of me is scared, but I'm excited too."

"I guess. With no plans, things are less predictable."

"True, but I can argue that the future itself is unpredictable for everyone no matter how many plans one makes," Mahesh claimed.

"Right," Aarvi agreed. Although she understood his point, she could never fathom leaving her family and India for such a long period. She wondered whether it was something that she was programmed to believe or whether Mahesh was being selfish in going against his parents' wishes. Had she not spoken to him and gotten to know him, she would have thought the latter.

The train hurtled past the railway crossing and slowly, the convoy of vehicles started moving. Within half an hour, they were a few streets away from the bookshop. A large procession of pilgrims again brought their car to a standstill. They decided to walk the rest of the way.

Once they reached the bookstore, Mahesh turned to Aarvi. "I am glad we made the trip. I enjoyed it."

"So did I," Aarvi said.

"Are you up for visiting Bhanu and Deepika?"

"It will have to be tomorrow. I can't on Saturday. I will have to be home to help with preparations for the evening function. We also have guests arriving from out of town, and some of them will be staying with us. It wouldn't look good if the bride-to-be was absent on the day of the celebration."

"I understand. We will try to squeeze in both visits tomorrow. In any case, I will see you on Saturday evening. Once again, thanks for inviting me and Karan."

"You are most welcome," Aarvi said.

After chatting for a while longer, she headed back into the bookshop, and Mahesh walked back to the car. Aarvi found Tarun standing near the cashiers talking to some tourists. It was time for the two of them to head home. As she looked at her father, Aarvi contemplated what she had learned about him and Chitra. Tarun caught his daughter looking at him and waved her over. Although she was staring right at him, her mind was elsewhere.

When the customers had finally left, Tarun walked up to Aarvi, and they left the store to head home. Aarvi was not in a talkative mood, and Tarun didn't press her after she told him that she was tired from her trip.

* * *

When Mahesh arrived at the bookstore Friday morning, Aarvi was already there, marshaling employees regarding their various tasks. She was visibly tired. That was understandable. Indian weddings were a marathon with all sorts of ceremonies and functions before the actual event.

Once the activities in the store had been sorted out, Aarvi and Mahesh headed to Sarnath to find Officer Bhanu Dev. They hoped he would be there and could help them understand why he had popped up in the cryptic clues. There wasn't much else to go on, as no one seemed to know Bhanu that well. The drive to Sarnath didn't take long.

Situated ten kilometers north of Benares, Sarnath was a popular tourist destination. Its claim to fame was that Buddha had taught spirituality there and spoke about his journey toward the path to enlightenment. It also housed some architectural wonders from the time of Ashoka the Great. Aarvi was quieter than usual, and although they spoke about Sarnath's history, Mahesh could sense her mind was elsewhere.

"Tired?" he asked once they reached the outskirts of Sarnath.

"Yes. Some guests arrived yesterday, and things in our house are chaotic," Aarvi muttered.

"I am surprised you could get away."

"Oh, trust me, that required quite an effort. Honestly, I am happy to get away for a bit. Once I get back, it will be one thing after another."

"Hopefully, things won't take long today, and you can go home early and rest."

"Oh, this outing is a rest for me. It's far more relaxing than being home right now. My uncle and his family arrived a day early from Madras. They are going to stay with us, and tonight, we have my aunt from Bombay arriving with her entourage, some of whom are also putting up with us. Suddenly, our home looks like a schoolyard full of rowdy kids," Aarvi stated loudly.

"I am guessing it's fun, too."

"Some of it is, yes, especially for my mom. She likes these big, chaotic get-togethers. She also likes to whine about them. I think that's part of her charm," Aarvi said, and they both laughed.

The large Ambassador had now stopped at an intersection in Sarnath. The driver rolled down his window and asked a rickshaw puller for directions to the police station. It wasn't hard to find, and after a few minutes, they were parked across the station that stood beside the Sarnath Museum. Established in 1904, predating India's independence, it housed a vast collection of Buddhist sculptures and scriptures. The most impressive exhibits belonged to the era of Ashoka the Great and his descendants. Some of the oldest artifacts were from the third century BC.

The police station, with its modern facade, looked out of place beside the museum. Mahesh wondered whether the city planners had considered how strange the buildings would look next to one another when they were setting out the plans.

Walking through the big iron gates of the station, they stepped into a large parking lot meant for police vehicles. Things were currently quiet. The station itself was a large, two-story building with a reception area and courtyard on the ground floor. Behind it were rooms for the officers and constables, and on the opposite side, behind a set of closed doors and gates, was a holding area for miscreants.

The upper floor was dedicated to the support staff and housed a canteen for the employees. The dark, foreboding interior of the station stood in stark contrast to the bright, sunny exterior. The fluorescent lighting gave it the appearance of a run-down factory.

Once they reached reception, they inquired about Bhanu Dev. A constable told them that he hadn't arrived yet, but they could see another officer on duty. Aarvi and Mahesh informed him that they would prefer to wait and were asked to sit on one of the long, uncomfortable wooden benches along the wall. While they waited, someone stopped by to inquire why they were there and then left them alone.

Nearly an hour later, an officer walked into the station. He seemed out of place in the building, dressed impeccably with a shiny belt and matching shoes. He stopped at reception, and the constable whispered something to him while pointing toward Aarvi and Mahesh. He glanced at them, and after chatting with the constable briefly, walked up to where they sat. They immediately got up and introduced themselves. He shook hands with them and escorted them to his office at the end of a long corridor.

The room was well lit with a large window. A desk stood on one side and a sitting area with sofas, chairs, and a coffee table on the other. The sparse furniture and bright decor made the compact room appear bigger. He spoke to his constable for a few minutes and then turned to them. "Would you like some tea?" Bhanu Dev asked.

"No, sir. Thank you," Aarvi and Mahesh replied.

Once the constable disappeared into the corridor, Bhanu gently closed the door, walked back to his comfortable chair, and settled in. The room seemed like an oasis compared with the hustle and bustle outside, and closing the door drowned out much of the noise.

Bhanu scrutinized Aarvi and then Mahesh. "How did you know the professor?"

They spent the next few minutes taking turns explaining their interaction with Devesh and what they knew about him. While they were talking, the phone on his desk rang. Bhanu asked them to pause while he spoke on the phone. After hanging up, he called for one of the constables who was sitting outside. He told the man, "Please request my secretary to hold all my calls unless it's urgent." Then he turned to Aarvi and motioned for her to continue.

Once Aarvi and Mahesh had finished, the officer sat silently with his hands folded in front of his mouth. Mahesh and Aarvi glanced at each other, unsure of what to do next. It was hard to read Bhanu Dev. His face, though pleasant, unlike most police officers they saw in the station, didn't carry much of an expression.

After a minute or so, Mahesh decided to break the silence. "Sir, if you don't mind my asking, how well did you know the professor?"

"I knew him. I can't say that I knew him well. He was my professor while I was studying in Delhi. At the time, we bonded since we were both from Benares. We spoke a lot about our hometown."

"And afterward?" Mahesh pressed.

"Sadly, I didn't keep in touch. Work took over, and I got busy. Also, I was not posted in Delhi, although that's not an excuse. I could have visited him during my trips there. But that didn't happen."

"And when he came back to Benares after his retirement?"

"He did reach out to me a month after he had arrived. I met him at his residence a couple of times. It's not far from here. He lives . . . lived in a neighborhood between Benares and Sarnath," Bhanu replied.

"This was before his accident?" Mahesh asked.

"Sorry?"

"What I meant, sir, is that you met him before his accident?"

"Ah yes, that's right. This was before his mishap. After that, I tried calling him to see if I could visit, but he was still recovering. I thought I'd give him time to recover before meeting him again," Bhanu said.

Mahesh leaned forward in his chair. "Sir, did you talk to him about his accident?"

"Right. This is where I am going to ask some questions. Normally, I wouldn't do this. It's rare for me to entertain people unannounced to talk about this sort of thing. But the professor was a good man. There was a time when I was struggling in college, and he helped me. I valued his guidance, and I do owe him more than my gratitude. Sadly, I couldn't do much. So, tell me, why are you here?"

Aarvi gestured for Mahesh to explain everything. Once again, he launched into a monologue with a captive audience, relaying the whole story starting with the crossword puzzles, what they learned after solving them, their trip to Jaunpur, and the news articles written by Deepika Roy, whom they still hadn't met. He left out the part where they suspected that Devesh and Mira had had a child out of wedlock and that Devesh may not have known about his daughter. He figured that was not the reason why the professor had sent them to Bhanu. Once

Mahesh had finished, he looked at Aarvi to see if she wanted to add anything.

"Sir, I think the professor suspected that his accident was premeditated and that most likely and we are not certain that his nephew and niece-in-law, Laxman and Rani, may have had something to do with his untimely death," Aarvi said, summarizing their point.

"But from what I heard, you think there are other suspects too," Bhanu contended.

"Certainly. Devesh's clues pointed us to Kulwant, the professor's servant. Laxman and Rani suggested that Kulwant was not giving medicines in a timely manner to the professor. And then Kulwant told us that Devesh Uncle had asked Hari Uncle for help, but never got a response. Then there was this new doctor who was Laxman's tenant before and was treating Devesh Uncle. I mean, why change doctors? Finally, there's Mangal Kumar's clerk, who earlier worked in Laxman's company. Why didn't he hand over the will right away? There are too many unanswered questions," Aarvi concluded.

"And a growing list of suspects," Bhanu added, leaning forward.

"Right, sir. The biggest reason we think that his death was untimely, was the Devesh Uncle himself stated as much in the clues he left for us. He knew his life was in danger," Aarvi concluded.

"Yes, I think I get that. I am just surprised that he never found a way to convey his fears and apprehensions to any of his friends or even the police," Bhanu said thoughtfully.

"He must have tried, but it was difficult," Aarvi responded. "We only know what we could decipher from the things he left us."

"Let me ask you, what do *you* believe? I mean there are lots of suspects, but you still think it's Laxman and Rani." Bhanu asked, looking at them. Aarvi nudged Mahesh to respond.

"Sir, if it was one thing, then we would have probably set it aside. But when you look at all the factors together, I think it's worth looking into. Moving the professor to the upper floor in a room where there were no phones, restricting visits from anyone, never leaving his side when he went out, and then what his loyal servant said about Laxman and Rani. Something's not right," Mahesh insisted.

"And the motive?" Bhanu asked, shuffling some papers on his desk.

"Laxman's financial problems may have been the trigger. Kulwant told us that the professor had given him a sealed envelope to be delivered to a lawyer, Mangal Kumar. We believe he may have wanted to change his will. Laxman needs money and is the sole beneficiary of his uncle's will. Plus, he partly owns a construction company that has trucks," Mahesh said.

"Hmm. Well, I really don't know what to say. I think what we have here may not be enough to open an investigation unless there is a formal first information report of any wrongdoing with some evidence. This may not hold up," Bhanu said and then grew silent.

Mahesh couldn't figure out whether he was still trying to absorb what he had just heard or had lost interest. Sharing a glance with Aarvi, he decided to press further. "I am sorry, I don't understand, sir," Mahesh pleaded. "Isn't the investigation into his accident still open? They never caught the driver who hit him."

"That's right, it is still open—officially. But as you know, it's been months since that incident. We have interviewed neighbors, drivers in the area, and many others, and we got nowhere. There are hundreds of trucks on the road in Benares at any time, and many of them are just passing through. We contacted the major trucking companies in the area, and from what I know, there were no leads."

Aarvi joined in. "Sorry, sir. I don't mean to pry, but you said from what you know?"

"When the accident happened, I wasn't here. I was on leave, on an extended vacation with my family. I came back after three weeks and learned of the mishap. One of my colleagues in the station was investigating. Although it was his investigation, he did keep me apprised of what was going on due to my interest in the case. There was nothing to suggest that it was anything other than a hit-and-run."

"Sir, didn't the accident strike you as rather odd since trucks don't frequent the area and the road where he was hit is usually deserted at that time of night?" Mahesh asked.

"Good point. I am impressed with how deeply you have investigated all this. Sadly, there isn't much else to go on unless something new comes up. Before you ask, everything that you have told me today is interesting, and I do appreciate your coming here to share it with me. However, I really can't open an investigation based on clues provided via crossword puzzles. Moreover, as I said before, we did investigate the hit-and-run, and unfortunately, we have been unable to catch the culprit," Bhanu said firmly.

Aarvi and Mahesh looked at each other, deflated.

Mahesh muttered, "We understand, sir. It's not the outcome we were expecting, but we knew coming here was a long shot. The only reason we're here is because the professor pointed us to you specifically. I am sure he felt that you would have done more if you could."

"I know. I wish I had learned about this earlier. It would have certainly helped in looking into his death."

"I am sorry, sir, I don't understand," Mahesh said. "Didn't you look into how he died?"

"From what I know, he was not in good health, and he had been deteriorating," Bhanu responded.

"How exactly did he die?" Mahesh asked. He knew the answer, but wanted to see if Bhanu could offer more details.

"A heart attack, I believe, precipitated by his condition. And from what I heard, a side effect from the pills he was taking," Bhanu stated.

"There was no postmortem done?"

"No, there was no reason for it. His death was not ruled suspicious. I mean, the hit-and-run was, but not his heart attack," Bhanu added.

Aarvi and Mahesh shared a knowing glance. Bhanu was again lost in thought, and Mahesh hoped he was wondering if the police had missed something.

Aarvi turned to Bhanu. "Sir, didn't you visit the professor's home after his passing?"

"No, actually, I was in Delhi on an official visit. I only came to know after I returned, a week after he'd died. I met Laxman and Rani to offer my condolences. Honestly, they seemed genuinely sad, and there was nothing to indicate that his death was anything but natural."

"Yet it does seem strange, sir, doesn't it?" Aarvi asked.

"What?"

"Both his accident and death happened while you were not in town. The one person who would have probably taken more of an interest was away during both incidents," pressed Aarvi.

"Now, wait a minute. You may be reading too much into this. Remember, the professor's clues didn't point to any concrete evidence. He didn't back up why he thought he was going to be killed," Bhanu asserted.

"There was no postmortem. Now it's too late," Aarvi snapped, her tone taking on a cutting edge.

Mahesh looked to Bhanu to see if the officer felt that she was being rude. Bhanu was staring into space. A silence hung over the group, and Mahesh could sense that Bhanu was absorbing everything that had transpired.

A constable knocked on the door before approaching Bhanu with some files and whispering something in his ear. Bhanu turned to them, and Mahesh sensed that was their cue to leave. "I am sorry to have to do this. But is there anything else you wish to add? Otherwise, I have other pressing matters to look into."

"No, sir," Mahesh replied, and Aarvi agreed.

"I know it's not the outcome you'd hoped for. The professor was a good man. I can see that he selected the right people to leave his papers and clues to," Bhanu said with a smile, getting up.

"Thank you for taking the time to meet us, sir," Aarvi said as they all shook hands.

Bhanu opened the door for them, and Aarvi and Mahesh dragged their feet down the long corridor to the exit and then past the gate. They were quiet, feeling disappointed with Bhanu's reaction.

Before getting into the car, Aarvi turned to Mahesh. "Doesn't seem like he is going to do anything," she said with a sigh.

"I am not so sure," Mahesh said, rubbing his chin in thought.

"What do you mean? You just heard. There wasn't enough to open an investigation."

"True. It could well be that he didn't want us to think he would investigate."

"But he clearly said someone needs to lodge an FIR."

"He doesn't need one. The hit-and-run case is still open. He could use that to continue looking into this."

Aarvi crossed her arms. "Why didn't he just tell us, then?"

"I don't know," Mahesh responded. "It could well be that he wants everyone to think this is over, maybe get Laxman and Rani to let their guard down. I'm not sure. He was difficult to read. On the other hand, you could be right. Maybe he won't do anything at all."

"But you feel otherwise?"

"That's what my gut says, based on the fact that the professor sent us to him and no one else. He seems to have sent clues to people who follow through and want answers. What do you think?" Mahesh asked with a smile.

Aarvi couldn't help but laugh. That lightened the mood as they got into the car and started toward the offices of *The Benares Examiner* to meet Deepika Roy.

* * *

A Poet's Ballad, A Crossword Mystery

Bhanu Dev sat silently in his chair, his arms folded and eyes closed. The phone on his desk rang, but he didn't pick up. After a few minutes, he opened his eyes and called for his constable. By the time he came in, Bhanu had risen from his chair and was preparing to leave, his face hard and determined. Before the constable could ask anything, he swung to face him.

"I need you to bring me the file on Professor Devesh Tripathi's hit-and-run case and leave it on my table."

"But sir, that case file is in the storage room with all the cold cases. It's been months now," the constable replied with a look of surprise.

"I understand, but I want to take another look. You worked on the case as well, didn't you?"

"Yes, sir," the constable confirmed.

"Good. Do you know where Laxman Tripathi works? The professor's nephew."

"Yes, he has a construction company on the other side of town. Do you want me to contact them?"

"Find out which lorry companies they use for transporting their goods," Bhanu ordered. "If they use their own trucks, I need the details of the drivers who were on the road on the day the professor was killed. I know some of that may be in the file, but I want to check if we missed anything or anyone."

"Sure, sir."

"Something isn't sitting right with me . . .," Bhanu started and then abruptly stopped.

"Anything else, sir?"

"Yes," Bhanu responded, looking at the constable.

"Sir?"

"Ask my driver to bring the Jeep around. You will be joining me as well."

"Where are we going, sir?"

"To meet the doctor who treated the professor after his accident and the one who signed off on his death certificate."

"Yes, sir," the constable responded. The tone in Bhanu's voice was clear enough—he didn't want any follow-up questions.

"Another thing."

"Sir?"

"I want you to find out the address of a lawyer, Mangal Kumar. He must be in the phone book. We will pay him a visit as well."

"Sure, sir," the constable replied quickly and turned slightly to make a quick exit before Bhanu started speaking again.

"One last thing," commanded Bhanu.

"Sir?"

"This stays between us. I know this wasn't my case. I just want to make sure that we have all the details and have left no stone unturned. Is that clear?"

"Understood, sir," the constable replied.

Bhanu nodded slightly, and the constable left the room.

* * *

The office of *The Benares Examiner* stood on the outskirts of the city, far from the tourist spots and posh neighborhoods. It was situated in an industrial area filled with small factories and warehouses. Their car stopped in front of a nondescript, four-story building. The paint on the facade was almost completely chipped away, and in some patches, the brick and cement were exposed. The pathway leading up to the building was not paved, and overgrown grass and weeds rose on either side.

A wooden board on the ground floor showed the names of all the firms that had offices in the building. It was hard to make out the details, since most of the lettering had worn off. From what was left, they could see that the office of *The Benares Examiner* was located on the third floor. Before taking the stairs, they quickly glanced toward the side of the wall that held the elevators. The lifts were completely dark, and there was a notice stating that they were out of order.

As they climbed the stairs, the clamor of other offices' occupants echoed when they crossed each floor. The floors seemed to be storage facilities for other companies. A few occupants who were coming down the stairs stared at them. Aarvi realized they probably stood out in this environment. The stairs and landings were piled with paper and dust. Some lights were not working, some were flickering, and cigarette butts and wrappers of all sorts littered the floor.

Once they reached the third floor, they could see entrances to offices on either side. One side was completely dark and empty. The other side had a small iron gate with a broken glass door behind it. Through the door, they could see several people and hear a cacophony of noises. Once they were inside, it was utter chaos. There was no reception area or front desk. The office looked like a giant, unkempt hall, with old, rickety desks and chairs of all shapes and sizes not arranged in any particular manner. Everything in the office seemed to make sounds—the old fans on the ceiling, the lights on the wall, the shutters on the windows, and a noisy water cooler in one corner struggling to stay alive.

Most desks held ancient, noisy typewriters and files that were falling over. Manning those desks were employees of all ages, ranging from scrawny twenty-year-olds with pocked faces to elderly men whose fat rolls draped over the arms of their chairs. A few were barking orders and smoking at the same time. They all seemed extremely busy and hardly noticed Aarvi and Mahesh. Some stared at them momentarily and then went back to their work. Aarvi wasn't sure what to do next, and from Mahesh's lost expression, neither was he.

They surveyed the room for a woman, hoping that it would be Deepika Roy. There were a few women working in one corner. Aarvi and Mahesh slowly shuffled toward that area, but were intercepted midway by an older gentleman wearing a deep-set scowl. After exchanging a few words, he pointed them toward a desk in one corner where a woman was seated with her back to them. She was on the phone. They walked toward her desk, patiently waiting for her to finish her conversation. Still holding the bulky phone to her ear, she turned around and noticed them looking at her. Before she could wave them over, a few of her colleagues started crowding her desk and asking her questions while she was still on the phone.

Aarvi and Mahesh shared an exasperated look, wondering whether they would ever get to talk to her in such a chaotic office. Aarvi looked around, not seeing any conference rooms. The *clickety-clack* of the typewriters and people talking over one another would make it impossible to have any meaningful conversation.

A Poet's Ballad, A Crossword Mystery

Once Deepika's colleagues left, Aarvi and Mahesh introduced themselves. She got up, shook their hands, and pointed at the end of the office toward the stairs. They followed her out of the office, down the stairs, and out of the building. She led them to a small makeshift tea stall. They ordered tea and then sat down on some uncomfortable stools across an elevated, upside-down wooden crate that acted as a table. Aarvi was relieved to be outside.

They could now get a full view of Deepika Roy in the sunlight. She looked to be in her late thirties, older than she probably was. She appeared tired and stressed, with deep bags under her eyes. But unlike the rest of her coworkers, she was well dressed and looked smart. After exchanging a few more pleasantries, it was Deepika who asked Aarvi and Mahesh about the professor first, "do you mind if I ask you which articles the professor left for both of you?"

"Sure," Mahesh replied, pulling out a sheaf of papers from his bag and handing them over to Deepika. Aarvi reached into her purse and did the same.

Deepika quickly glanced at them and then handed them back. "All the newspaper cuttings were articles written by me? There was nothing else?" she asked, visibly confused.

Aarvi and Mahesh looked at each other. Aarvi knew they had to tell Deepika more about the puzzles. Aarvi quickly summarized everything, leaving out the bit about Devesh's daughter.

"Wow, this is interesting," Deepika said thoughtfully.

"Ma'am, how well did you know the professor?" Aarvi asked.

"Not that well. He is the one who actually contacted us once he returned from Delhi. He was very keen that we publish crosswords in our paper and said he would help us with it."

"Did you?" Mahesh asked.

"What?"

"Publish any of his crosswords."

"I couldn't get the owners of my paper to agree. As you may have sensed, our paper isn't exactly thriving.

It doesn't have great circulation and isn't doing well financially. It wasn't always like this, you know. When I joined ten years ago, it held a lot of promise, and we started with a bang. Then there was a change in ownership and management three years ago. It went downhill from there. We used to occupy three floors of this building. We went from over three hundred employees to just seventy," Deepika said and let out a heavy sigh.

"Oh, I am sorry to hear that," Mahesh said quickly, bouncing his knees impatiently. They weren't there for a rundown on the health of the newspaper. Since his time was running short, Aarvi realized Mahesh was getting jittery, but he didn't want to come across as curt. He waited for a few seconds and then pressed further. "Did he actually send any puzzles to you?"

"No, he didn't."

"If you don't mind my asking, ma'am, when was the last time you spoke to him?"

"Oh, that was months ago, just after his accident. He sent his servant to our office—I forget his name—to ask us to continue his subscription to our paper. I am not sure why he liked this paper so much."

"Kulwant?" Mahesh prodded.

"Sorry?"

"The name of his servant, was it Kulwant?" Mahesh asked.

"I can't say for sure, perhaps. I came to know from my colleague that he had come by to see me. He had left a note from Devesh and payment for the subscription."

"What did the note say?" Mahesh continued fervently.

"I am not sure," Deepika mumbled.

"What do you mean?" Mahesh demanded.

"I was away for a couple of days, and when I came back, I was told about the subscription and the note. As you can see, our office is a mess. I never followed up on the note. I did call the professor at home to thank him, but he was unavailable. I tried again a couple of times and ended up speaking to his nephew. I stopped after that."

"Laxman?"

"Yes, that's right. I remember talking to him," Deepika confirmed.

Mahesh paused. "Ma'am, what did Laxman say each time you wanted to speak to the professor?"

"That he was resting or sleeping," Deepika murmured. Aarvi could see that she was playing out all the responses in her head based on what they had told her. Aarvi, who had been quiet for a while, leaned in to ask, "Ma'am, when did you come to know of his death?"

"A couple of weeks after he passed away," Deepika responded. "One of my colleagues called him to let him know that his subscription was up for renewal. He was informed that the professor had died of a heart attack. I called the family to offer my condolences."

"I am sorry, ma'am, if this sounds a bit odd, but do you have any idea why he left newspaper cuttings authored by you with us? We are at a loss," Aarvi said, fidgeting with her cup.

Deepika stretched out her hand, indicating that she wanted to look at the articles again. They handed the papers over to her. After a few minutes, she had a puzzled look on her face. She scrutinized them once more before handing them back to Aarvi and Mahesh.

"I have to say there's something strange here," Deepika said, enunciating each word slowly.

"Yes, ma'am. All this is rather weird," Mahesh agreed.

"No, not just everything you have told me, but all the articles you showed me."

"What?" Aarvi and Mahesh asked, their voices overlapping.

"As you can see, I have written many articles on various topics. We are a small newspaper, after all, and all of us wear several hats. We don't have the luxury of having dedicated journalists for different areas."

"Right," Aarvi responded eagerly, trying to prod Deepika to get to the point faster.

"The one article that made me somewhat famous among my peers, and made others take notice of our paper, is not here," Deepika noted, furrowing her brow.

"What was it about?"

"Illegal dumping of waste in the forests around Benares by construction companies," Deepika said and paused.

Aarvi and Mahesh were speechless. They looked at each other. Aarvi nodded slightly, urging Mahesh to continue.

"Did one of the companies that you looked into belong to the professor's nephew, Laxman? He is a co-owner of a construction company."

"I know," Deepika said. "But I didn't interview him. Most of the owners didn't want to deal with the press on an issue that portrayed them in a bad light. Usually, they would ask one of the managers to meet with us and give us vague responses. I think that's what happened with Laxman's company, too."

"Did you look into his company's finances?"

"No, that was not the focus of the article," Deepika replied.

"What happened after you published it?"

"It was heralded by the public and in the media, bringing us some much-needed accolades. But that was short-lived. I learned later that the owners of our paper were not too happy with the article since they have business interests with some of the same firms we investigated. They quietly moved me to other stories."

Mahesh leaned forward, having hardly touched his tea. "Is it possible that the professor sent us to you because of this missing article? He couldn't have included that in what he gave us. But he included other articles hoping that we would contact you and figure this out somehow."

"Figure what out?" Deepika asked.

"Ma'am, we can't say for sure what he wanted. But everything that we have uncovered so far has led us to people like yourself. People who, I think, will look into his mishap."

"That's a bit of a stretch, don't you think?" Deepika asked, sounding unsure.

"Why else would he send us to you? I can only assume he wanted someone to investigate his accident. I believe he sent us to a police officer and you, a journalist, for that reason."

"Hmm. You could be right. I don't know what to make of it. But I have to agree about looking into the finances of Laxman's company. Now, there is something I haven't told you," Deepika said, which piqued their interest.

"What's that?" Aarvi asked.

"Well, there was this old gentleman who came by a few weeks ago to talk to me about a book that had been left by the professor to his son. His son was a student at Delhi University. As you said, Devesh left books and other things to some of his students. Anyway, it seems that this gentleman read the book after his son had finished reading it and noticed several words underlined in various chapters. Now, I don't remember the name of the book or the gentleman. What I do remember is that he was certain the words added up to a message or phrases that pointed to financial irregularities by a relative that resulted in a murder," Deepika said, looking at Mahesh and then at Aarvi.

Aarvi nearly spilled her tea in her shock. "What did you do?"

"Nothing. There wasn't anything to go on. It didn't make any sense. I dismissed it as the vivid imagination of an old man and left it at that," Deepika responded.

"Why didn't he go to the police or another newspaper? Why you?"

"So that's the thing. When the old man deciphered the clues and phrases in the book, his interpretation was that it was meant for me."

"With that, and from what we have told you, are you convinced that the professor's accident and possibly his death may have been unnatural?" Aarvi asked.

"Convinced, no. But worthy of an investigation, certainly. I regret not taking the old man more seriously," Deepika stated, shaking her head.

"What will you do now?" Aarvi pressed.

"Now, I need to get back to my office," Deepika said and smiled for the first time. "Rest assured; I will find the note that Devesh sent me to see if it holds any clues. I will also find out more about the old man, his allegation, in light of what you have told me."

"Thank you, ma'am," Aarvi said, and Mahesh nodded. They were both satisfied with the answer.

Deepika gave Aarvi a scrutinizing look and grinned. "I know where I have seen you before. At the Sanskriti Bookshop. You work there, don't you?"

"Yes, ma'am. It belongs to my family," Aarvi replied with a smile.

"Oh, that's wonderful. Owning a bookstore and working there must be marvelous."

"It is," she said quietly.

"Well, I guess I will see you there during my next visit," Deepika said, shifting her stance slightly to get up.

"I am not sure, ma'am. I am getting married next weekend and then . . ."

"Oh, I see," Deepika said, glancing between them.

Before she could say anything, Aarvi quickly added, "Mahesh is going back to Delhi on Sunday. He is going to London next weekend for higher studies." She didn't want Deepika to assume, as Mira had in Jaunpur, that Mahesh was the one she was marrying.

"Congratulations to both of you on your new journeys."

"Thank you," they responded.

"Before I go, I do have one question. Who is the police officer in Sarnath that Devesh's clues sent you to?" Deepika asked.

"Bhanu Dev," Mahesh responded.

"Hmm. Well, he does have a bit of a reputation."

"What kind of reputation?" Aarvi inquired.

"He is a good officer, sees things through. I am not sure how much he will share with the press. But I can tell you that in that station, Bhanu Dev is the best officer."

Hearing that set Aarvi at ease, despite the fact that Bhanu hadn't given them any indication that he would pursue the case. After a brief pause, Deepika got up. Aarvi and Mahesh stood up to shake her hand. They exchanged a few parting words, and Deepika headed back to the building while Aarvi and Mahesh made their way back to the car. Once they settled in, Aarvi turned to Mahesh.

"The old man she was talking about wasn't Hari Das. He doesn't have a son, and Devesh Uncle didn't leave him any book with clues or else he would have told us."

"No, it's definitely not him," Mahesh said as the car started moving. "You know what this means?"

"What?"

He brought his eyes to hers. "It means the professor left a whole set of clues in books and papers that were given to many other people. I am not sure how many of them will realize what they are or whether any of them will take the time to solve them and follow through with their messages. But it looks like we weren't the only ones."

Ballad

On the drive back to the bookshop, Mahesh realized there was so much more to Devesh's story than what they had uncovered. What also preoccupied his thoughts was that they had now come to the end of their set of clues. There was nothing else to follow up on. Suddenly, there was a void.

As the car rolled toward Assi Ghat, they silently looked out the window. Aarvi turned to Mahesh after a few minutes.

"I guess this is it. We have solved all the clues," she said softly.

"I guess we have," he responded, noting a hint of dejection in her voice.

"Do you want to stop at a tea shop? I am a bit hungry. We can go to the one near the bookstore."

"Sure," Mahesh replied. "Do you think Deepika and Bhanu will follow up on what we have told them?"

"I don't know. I am hoping they do. As you said earlier, he seemed to have pointed us to people who he probably had some faith in."

"Faith that they would do something?"

She nodded.

"Like us," Mahesh declared.

"Perhaps. Don't you think that's the case?"

"I am not sure anymore. I feel that we could have done more and probably *should* do more. I don't know," Mahesh responded thoughtfully.

"I think we have taken it as far as we could. We have our own lives to lead, and we have left it, as the professor wanted, with the people he thought he could count on. Now it's up to them," Aarvi asserted.

"True," Mahesh said. The car veered into the crowded street leading up to the tea shop.

"You have to marvel at his ingenuity. He was alone, scared, yet he decided to leave a set of clues to so many people, hoping that someone may decipher them. This must have taken quite an effort and time. Doing all this without knowing how it would end must have left him frustrated and probably angry too."

"It is sad," Mahesh said with a sigh. "I can't imagine how lonely and scared he must have been. As for what prompted him to do this, well, I think it could have been desperation or revenge, or maybe both. We will never know."

Aarvi asked the driver to stop and park the car so they could walk the rest of the way. Although the streets were crowded, the eatery wasn't. They easily found a booth toward the end of the establishment and quickly ordered some samosas, lassi, and tea. Once they sat down, Mahesh realized that this was perhaps the last moment they would spend alone together.

"It has been quite a week, hasn't it?" Mahesh murmured with a wistful smile.

"It has," Aarvi murmured, placing her hands on the table.

"And a memorable one, too."

"Yes, the stuff we found out about Devesh Uncle's past, his love interest in college, his daughter out of wedlock, the fact that he may have been murdered, and of course, his poems. I honestly think they are good enough to be published, and I hope Mira does publish them."

"Oh no. Not just that," Mahesh whispered.

"Sorry?"

"I mean, those things made this trip exciting. What made it unforgettable was you, Aarvi," Mahesh said with a sad smile.

Before Aarvi could reply, the waiter came by, and they stopped talking. After he had served them, they both ate silently for the next few minutes.

"You must be tired," Aarvi said, looking at Mahesh.

"I am. Next week will be tiring too. I have finished most of my packing and preparations for my trip, but I'll be going around Delhi with my parents, and they will have a never-ending list of things to tell me and give me before I leave."

"That's understandable. Do you think you will see your mother differently now, given what you learned about her and my father?"

"I don't know. I have always seen my mom as my mom. She is always busy fretting over us, stressed about something or other. We tend to forget that our parents were young too and had a life before they became parents, and even before they got married," Mahesh said.

Aarvi shook her head slightly. "I can't ever imagine that my parents were in love with someone else during their school or college days. Honestly, I don't want to think about that, nor have I ever considered that they were capable of it. To think that my father and your mother were involved just seems so weird and foreign. I don't even know how to react."

"Right," Mahesh said, and before he could say anything more, a voice rose from one of the other tables in the small café.

"Aarvi, is that you?"

They turned around to see two elderly women who were getting up from a booth. Mahesh turned to Aarvi, who clearly wasn't happy to see them.

"Yes, aunty, it's me," Aarvi said with a hint of disappointment. Mahesh couldn't be sure, but he sensed some embarrassment in her voice, too.

"And who is this?" one of the old women asked, walking up to them. She was short, round, and intimidating. What bothered Mahesh was that she made Aarvi feel uncomfortable.

"My name is Mahesh—"

"This is Mahesh from Delhi. He is leaving the day after tomorrow," Aarvi snapped.

Mahesh was taken aback by not only her introduction but also her curt demeanor. He could sense that she did not want to have a prolonged conversation with these women. Then, Aarvi gestured to the woman and turned to Mahesh. "And this is Sheila Aunty, one of our closest family friends."

"Nice to meet you, ma'am," Mahesh said politely, with a weak smile.

"We are leaving soon. I have to meet my father at the bookstore and head home," Aarvi pronounced, making it clear once again that she didn't want to discuss anything further. That seemed to do the trick, and both women took the hint. Before leaving, Sheila turned to Aarvi.

"Well, your mother is going to be happy that you won't be spending time at that wretched store. God knows what Tarun sees in it. He could just sell it, invest the money in some rental property, and live really well. I heard that Ashish is not interested in it either. Now that you are getting married, what's the point in keeping it, I wonder?"

Mahesh noticed Aarvi's face tightening, her hands clutching her glass firmly, but she managed to keep outwardly calm. The waiter came by, and once the two women settled the bill, they strutted out of the café.

Aarvi had become quiet, and it was evident that the interaction with Sheila had upset her. Mahesh tried his best to calm things, but to no avail. They sat in silence, ate their snack, and finished their tea. They asked for the bill, and while they waited, Mahesh glanced at Aarvi, who was still flustered.

"You know, if it makes you feel any better, I have had my share of nosy aunties. The best thing is to ignore them," Mahesh suggested.

"You don't understand. You are a boy, and it's different for girls. Now that she has seen us, she is going to go about saying that she saw me with a boy a week before my wedding, and it's going to be the subject of juicy gossip. Never mind that I am getting married next weekend and you are off to another part of the world, and I am never going to see you again," Aarvi huffed.

"Is that why you introduced me that way?"

"What else could I have done?" Aarvi said curtly, still furious. "I couldn't have said that you are my friend and we have been going around this week trying to figure out what some crazy professor left us by way of clues."

"Well, it was more than that . . ."

"Really?" Aarvi's voice had become loud enough for other patrons to stare at them. She glared back at them, and they looked away. She turned back to Mahesh and lowered her voice, though it still trembled with anger. "What have we been doing, really? What good has all this done?"

"We don't know anything for sure," Mahesh responded in a gentler tone. He hadn't seen this side of

Aarvi. It was evident that there was more preying on her mind than she was letting on. Her expression was stern and worried.

"So what? We found out that he was in love in college, has a daughter whom he knew nothing about, and that he might have been killed. And, of course, he paired us up together because he figured out our parents were involved. What is that? Some kind of cosmic joke?" Aarvi blurted, her eyes taking on a menacing look.

"I think we did what we could. Giving the book to Mira, telling Hari Das about Devesh's will, letting Deepika and Bhanu know of his apprehensions. And yes, maybe he thought we would do this together, although he couldn't have known that for sure," Mahesh said, trying to calm Aarvi down. It didn't work.

"Maybe my mother is right. I should be focusing on my wedding rather than this meaningless stuff," Aarvi said, fixing her eyes on Mahesh.

He wondered whether she could see how this conversation cut him deeply, though he tried not to show it. He looked her in the eye, trying to understand why she was behaving this way. Instead, she looked away.

"It was also the right thing to do," Mahesh said, almost whispering.

"I am not sure about that," Aarvi growled, still averting her eyes.

Seeing that Aarvi was still angry and his efforts to calm her were not having any impact, Mahesh decided to change the subject. "I think she was wrong about the bookstore," he said.

"Why? She is right. No one expects me to work after my marriage."

"Things are changing."

"Maybe in your part of the world, Mahesh, but not here," Aarvi said, banging her forefinger on the table.

"Perhaps you can bring about that change in some small way," Mahesh added in a hushed tone.

"It's easy for you to say, isn't it? Someone who is just picking up and leaving!" she yelled. The other patrons at the establishment suddenly stopped what they were doing and glanced at Aarvi and Mahesh. Aarvi glared back at them, and after a long minute, they want back to what they were doing before.

Mahesh stared down at the table. "I didn't mean to upset you."

"I don't think you understand, Mahesh, really. It's easy for you to judge and preach what I should do. Trust me, it's not that simple."

"You are right, Aarvi. I don't understand. I can't possibly put myself in your shoes and comprehend the pressures that you have to deal with and the weight of expectations," Mahesh said, his understanding tone calming Aarvi down.

The waiter had come with the bill, and after Mahesh took care of it, they slowly walked to the bookstore. They stopped a few steps away from the entrance and could see the bright lights of the ghat on one side and the inside of the store through the large glass doors in front. The store looked busy. Tarun was standing near the doorway, chatting with some customers. Aarvi remained silent. A few yards away from the store, she stopped. Mahesh turned to face her.

"I think I will go from here on my own," Aarvi said softly.

"Sure," Mahesh said. He was somewhat surprised, but didn't want to argue.

"I know I invited you and Karan to come to our place tomorrow for the function," she said abruptly in a hushed tone.

"Yes," Mahesh said tentatively.

"I think it's best if you don't come. It's mostly for close friends and family, and things could be awkward," Aarvi said.

He forced a slight smile. "As you wish, Aarvi."

"I will be busy tomorrow," she said, her voice breaking. "I think it's time we went our own ways." With that, she turned and hustled toward the store before Mahesh could say anything.

He wanted to follow her, but he thought better of it. He could see her almost running into the store, and once she entered, she quickly disappeared toward the back, out of view.

Mahesh stood there for a minute or two, crestfallen. He kept staring at the bookstore, and then slowly turned and walked back to the car.

* * *

Aarvi knew that Saturday would be hectic. But she hadn't realized just how busy it would be. She had had a sleepless night, not only because of all the guests and wedding-related commotion in the house, but also because of how things had ended with Mahesh. Immediately after stepping into the store the evening before, she had felt terrible. Once she had regained some of her composure, she had gone back outside to find him. But he had left. Later that night, she had kept to herself amid a big family dinner with all her relatives who were staying with them. She had felt all alone.

She had tossed and turned in bed. So many guests in the house meant that she had to share her room with one of her cousins, which didn't help. Her relatives had been busy talking about and planning the wedding while Aarvi's mind had been elsewhere. Meanwhile, her parents and her brother had been busy catering to the needs of all the guests who were staying over. Everyone had seemed busy and strangely happier than Aarvi.

When Saturday morning rolled around, she awoke to the sound of Ritika and one of her aunts asking her to come down to the drawing room for a small puja. Most of the morning was spent getting things ready for the evening. After the short ceremony, there was yet another prolonged lunch with her relatives.

Aarvi was already exhausted. She wondered how she would get through the day, not to mention the main event in the evening. What bothered her most was that she had absolutely no time to herself. She wondered if she could call Mahesh at the guesthouse and apologize for her behavior. But the phone was constantly busy with someone on it barking orders for the evening's preparations.

Finally, in the afternoon, a few relatives decided to visit the ghats and temples. Since Aarvi was the star attraction of the evening show, she wasn't expected to join them. Tarun and Ashish divided up the guests into two cars and headed out. Ritika and an aunt stayed behind to make sure everything was in order for the party. Aarvi was worn out. Ritika asked her to go to her room and rest.

When the phone was finally free, Aarvi tried calling the guesthouse, but she couldn't reach Mahesh in his room. After several attempts, even pleading with the receptionist to check whether he was elsewhere on the property, she was finally informed that he had left after lunch with a friend. They weren't sure when he would be expected back.

He is probably out with Karan, Aarvi thought. She left her number with the guesthouse, requesting them to ask Mahesh to call her back when he returned. She knew there wasn't much of a chance of getting through to him.

Once back in her room, she felt her eyelids drooping. She tried to sleep but couldn't. Gazing out her large window, she could see the garden and courtyard outside getting decked up for the function. Thankfully, the weather was fair with no forecast of rain. As the workers went about their chores in the garden, she looked farther out. The roads were congested with people going about their business.

She sat back down on her bed and glanced toward her desk. She took out a notebook she had treasured since she had been a child—a collection of stories she had written over the years. No one knew of its existence except for the one clerk at the bookstore to whom she had entrusted the task of typing up a copy of the handwritten manuscript. She had sworn him to secrecy and had told him that she would be the one letting everyone know of the book when the time was right. He had been happy to oblige.

She stepped over to her bookshelf, carefully pulling out another notebook. This was the typewritten copy. She gently leafed through the stories and smiled. She went back to her bed, opened the book, and started reading.

After a couple of hours, the coterie that had left to see the sights and sounds of Benares were all back. The relative calm inside the house had been replaced by a constant drone of people talking over one another. Occasionally, there were raised voices shouting orders. Aarvi, as was expected of her, went down to have tea and snacks with them. They were excited to tell her about all the places they had visited and what they liked. Aarvi listened politely with a distant smile, once in a while engaging in some conversation.

The guests would start to arrive in a couple of hours. It was the norm during such parties for folks to show up fashionably late, but with so many relatives already in the house, it would take time for everyone to get ready. When

Aarvi went back to her room, she found Ritika, one of her aunts, and a cousin already there, laying out on her bed everything she was going to wear. There seemed to be an endless discussion of what she should be wearing, how she should look, and what type of jewelry and shoes would go with the attire that they had selected.

After an exhausting hour or so, they left Aarvi with some privacy to change and get ready. Once she was all decked out, she called for Ritika, who arrived with some aunts and cousins. They all marveled at how beautiful she looked, but Aarvi had already started sweating. A bride's attire and heavy jewelry were impractical for Indian summers. Ritika barked a few more orders, and some workers came up with a couple of huge fans and a makeshift cooler. That helped, but Aarvi was still uncomfortable.

Jeev and his parents arrived at 6:00 p.m., and everyone commented on how stunning the couple looked. Aarvi was happy to see Jeev, who pulled her aside, and the rest of their entourage gave them some privacy. Though they didn't have much time to themselves, it was better than having to engage in all the small talk and forced conversations with their relatives.

A Poet's Ballad, A Crossword Mystery

At around 7:00 p.m., a gentle breeze cloaked the evening in a comfortable coolness, and they headed outside. The gardens had been decked out with flowers, and a few makeshift gazebos had been erected with sofas and chairs for guests. Lights of different colors had been strung up, and once they were all illuminated, the setting was enchanting.

Aarvi and Jeev made their way to the most decorated gazebo with chairs that looked like thrones. Once they made themselves comfortable, there was a constant flow of relatives coming by to talk to them and ensure they had everything they needed. Soon, a flurry of guests started arriving. By 9:00 p.m., the house, courtyard, and garden were teeming with people. Aarvi felt a bit better after her friends arrived. The excitement momentarily took her mind off Mahesh. Still, she couldn't help but think that she would have enjoyed herself so much more had he been at the party.

Once the guests began eating their dinner at the round tables and in the seating areas, a band started playing at the dais that had been erected at one end of the garden. The food, drinks, and Bollywood music seemed to have the desired effect. Soon everyone forgot about their formal attire and inhibitions, and started swaying and dancing out of resonance with the music that was playing.

Aarvi's and Jeev's families seemed overjoyed that everybody was having a good time. Jeev was busy with some of his friends and colleagues from work. Aarvi occasionally talked to them, then moved to different tables to meet everyone.

At around midnight, the guests started trickling out. The relatives who were staying with the Lals also started making their way back into the house. Everyone seemed happy, well fed, and satisfied. Aarvi's parents were happy that the event had gone well. But it was obvious to Tarun and Aarvi that the ones who had enjoyed the evening the most were Ritika and Jeev's mother.

Once all the guests had left, Jeev and his parents spent a few minutes with Aarvi, Tarun, and Ritika. They seemed pleased and soon got up to leave. Tarun walked them back to their car while Ritika retreated inside for the evening.

* * *

Aarvi sat down on one of the large sofas in the empty garden. Some workers from the catering company had just finished cleaning up and were also retiring for the evening. The plan was to come back and dismantle everything the following morning.

When Tarun stepped through the gate after walking Jeev and his parents to their car, he saw Aarvi slumped on the sofa, looking tired, sad, and somewhat lost. His daughter's aloofness during the evening hadn't gone unnoticed. Tarun had asked Ritika about it, and she was convinced it was because she would miss home and her parents once she was married. He wasn't sure that was the only reason.

Slowly, he walked up to her and sat down beside her. Aarvi gave him an affectionate look and leaned her head on his shoulder as they sat side by side.

"You looked stunning today," Tarun said with a big smile.

"Is that your unbiased opinion?"

"Yes," he replied, happy to see a smile on his daughter's face. But it was a sad smile.

He cleared his throat. "Hari Das came by to talk to me."

"Oh, about what?" Aarvi asked, her tone changing suddenly.

"About what you and Mahesh uncovered concerning Devesh. He told me that he was proud of what you did. You know Hari regrets that he couldn't help Devesh more when he was alive. He got caught up chasing other things, which were not important."

"Hari Uncle is a good man," Aarvi said, surprising Tarun. She had never talked to him about Hari.

"He is," Tarun agreed.

"He's not as crazy as people make him out to be."

"No, he isn't."

"He was also a good friend to Devesh Uncle. Even now, he is trying his best to do right by him. I wish I had friends like that," Aarvi said with a soft sigh.

"Speaking of Devesh, Hari told me something strange today."

"What's that?" Aarvi asked, perking up.

"He is trying to get in touch with the lawyer who drew up Devesh's will. Hari doesn't know all the details just yet, but it seems that Devesh may have instructed his lawyer to change his will and not bequeath everything to Laxman and Rani."

"Oh. Did he say who the new beneficiaries were?" Aarvi inquired.

"Well, that's the strange part. Hari is following up on that, but it could be someone in Jaunpur."

"Wow . . ." Aarvi said, suddenly growing quiet. Tarun wondered if her trip to Jaunpur with Mahesh had had anything to do with all this.

"You know, ever since you were a little girl, there was one thing that I could always make out," Tarun said, looking at her lovingly.

"What's that?" Aarvi asked in a tired voice.

"No matter how busy or preoccupied we were, I always knew when my daughter was unhappy or if there was something on her mind."

"What makes you say that?"

"I have seen you all evening. You have been distant. Yes, there have been moments when you have enjoyed yourself. But I have also seen you somewhat sad. What's going on, Aarvi?"

"It's nothing, really . . . ," she started.

"I asked your mother, and she told me that it could be because you are coming to the realization that you'll be leaving us and starting a new life. She thinks that maybe it's because you will miss what you are used to," Tarun said.

"And you don't think that's the case?"

"No, I don't."

"What do you think?" Aarvi asked, her head still resting on her father's shoulder.

"At first, I thought it may be because you would miss coming to the bookstore. I know you like working there very much. But I am not sure that's it."

"So, what do you think now?"

"Does it have anything to do with Mahesh? I thought you invited him and his friend. Why didn't they come?

I thought he was leaving for Delhi tomorrow. They could have still come tonight."

"They couldn't come," Aarvi said softly.

"That's strange. I thought he would have enjoyed coming here," Tarun asserted.

"Maybe. I guess now we won't know."

"Did he tell you why he wasn't able to make it?"

"No."

"And you still didn't answer my question," Tarun went on.

"What's that?" Aarvi asked.

"Was it his absence at the party or something about him that made you sad?" Tarun asked.

Aarvi sat upright and then turned to face him. She wrapped her arms around him and started crying. Tarun tried to console her as they embraced. She leaned back and looked at him, her cheeks wet from the tears rolling down her face.

Finally, after regaining some composure, she said, "I asked him not to come."

"Why on earth would you do that? I thought you liked him."

"I do," Aarvi said.

"Tell me what's going on," Tarun pleaded.

Aarvi nodded and then told him everything that had happened that week, leaving nothing out. He listened without interruption or judgment. Once she finished, fresh tears started rolling down her face.

Tarun smiled at her and then took her in his arms, giving her a long, affectionate hug. He remembered having long chats with Aarvi when she was in school. As she had grown older, they had gradually become fewer and fewer. The discussions would sometimes turn into arguments, and Tarun had sensed that Aarvi had wanted to avoid those. He was glad that she was able to unload what was on her mind and hoped that she felt much better after their long conversation, something they hadn't had in a very long time.

It was nearly 2:00 a.m. when they finished talking. The gentle breeze was cool and refreshing. Everyone in the house was fast asleep, and most of the lights had been shut off. Aarvi slowly got up to head back into the house. Before leaving Tarun, she turned to him. "Why did you think it had anything to do with Mahesh?" she asked.

"What do you mean?" Tarun asked.

"I know you know me, and you are perceptive. But what made you think that Mahesh was on my mind this evening?"

"One of the servants came and told me that he had called from the guesthouse."

"Oh, why didn't they come to get me?"

"You were busy, and we weren't entertaining any calls. Your mother and I instructed everyone picking up the phone to take down their name and number and let them know that we would call them back. We couldn't have possibly dragged you away from all the guests to pick up a call," Tarun replied.

"Right," Aarvi said with a sigh. "Was there anything else?"

"It seems he came by and left you a gift."

"Who? Mahesh?" she asked suddenly, her voice rising in volume. "Why wasn't I told? I didn't see him."

"Easy, Aarvi. He came by early in the evening when you were getting ready in your room. He left the gift downstairs with one of the servants with a note that they should hand it over to you. I guess, given what you told him yesterday, he figured you didn't want to see him."

"Oh," Aarvi said, sounding dejected. Tarun could sense from the pained look on her face that she felt miserable.

"Are you all right?"

"Where's the gift?" she asked.

"I had it sent to your room. It should be on your desk."

"Thank you . . . good night," Aarvi whispered and gave Tarun a hug.

"Good night," Tarun said, watching his daughter enter the house. Once she was inside, he reached into his pocket. He had been yearning to do this all night and finally had a moment to himself. He pulled out a cigarette from the pack that was well hidden in his attire and started smoking.

* * *

When Aarvi reached her room, she gently opened the door. Her cousin was fast asleep on one side of the bed, snoring loudly. She lit a small night lamp and tiptoed to the desk. There, she found a small package. She opened it, and a handwritten note fell out. It was from Mahesh, wishing her and Jeev well on their union. Her eyes fell upon a beautifully crafted filigree notebook.

She felt a lump in her throat, and her eyes welled up. She glanced toward her bed to make sure that her cousin was still sleeping and didn't catch her reaction. Satisfied, she held the exquisitely embroidered notebook close to the lamp and marveled at the intricate design on the cover, spine, and back. The pages were smooth and shiny.

She was about to put away the packaging when she felt something else inside the wrapping paper. She carefully reached in to find a beautiful handmade wooden pen. She held it close to the lamp to view its design and noticed that her name was engraved on it.

She held both gifts for a while and then gently placed them back on her desk. Mahesh's thoughtful gifts made her heart swell, but the fact that she hadn't seen him tonight saddened her.

She changed and got ready for bed. Before turning in for the night, she went to open the window in her room overlooking the garden. She opened it and looked out, seeing a dark sky full of stars. Then her gaze shifted down toward the garden where Tarun was enjoying a smoke while looking up at the stars.

* * *

On Saturday morning, Mahesh's alarm woke him up at 5:00 a.m. There wasn't much to pack. Karan had already arrived, insisting that he would drop him off at the station. Mahesh headed to the lobby to ask the receptionist if they could get some tea at this hour. They quickly got hold of some kitchen staff who had come in to prepare breakfast.

When Mahesh came down to settle the bill for his stay, Karan flatly refused. He had already taken care of it. Mahesh had suspected that he might do something like this. True to his name, Karan was known for his generosity and friendship. They hastily finished their tea and made their way to Karan's car.

Traffic at this hour was light, and the drive revealed a different side of this old, majestic town. As they passed some of the temples and ghats and drove across the Ganges, Mahesh couldn't help but wonder whether he would ever return. Karan was right. Once he was busy with his life abroad, moments spent in places like these would be relegated to his memories.

They reached the station with fifteen minutes left before the train to Delhi was departing. At this hour, the train was not that crowded, and while Karan waited on the platform, Mahesh went inside with his ticket to check his allocated berth on the coach. He left his bag under the watchful eye of a fellow passenger and then headed back outside to bid Karan farewell. When he stepped outside, he noticed Karan talking to one of the porters, asking him whether the train would be leaving on time. Usually, morning trains that started from the point of origin were not late.

"All good?" Karan asked as Mahesh hopped back down from the train.

"Yes," he said, stepping away from the door of the coach to allow other passengers to get in. They stood on the platform facing the train, a sadness hanging between them.

"Well, next weekend you have a longer journey," Karan said.

"I do," Mahesh replied softly. "I don't know where that's going to lead."

"Listen, Mahesh, I know you. You will try your best, and you have always wanted this."

"Yes, and I know if I don't go, I will regret not taking the opportunity. B-b-but . . ." Mahesh stammered.

"Where's this coming from? I always thought you were a confident fellow. I can understand that you are going far away and will miss home. But you are not having second thoughts, are you?"

"No, I'm not. But much of the confidence that I usually portray is a facade. I am going through a range of emotions at the moment—sadness, excitement, dread, all rolled into a curry," Mahesh said, managing a weak smile.

"I can't say I understand. But I do wish you luck, my friend. Somehow I get the feeling that things will work out in your favor in the end. You will find your way."

"Thank you, Karan."

"Give me a call before you leave. I'm sure you will be busy. I know I am. But please try to keep in touch."

"I will, Karan. I want to thank you for your hospitality."

"Oh, come off it. No need for that between friends."

"Still, I will miss my friends, you know."

"Yes, and you will make new ones. Who knows? There might actually be a girl in London that you fancy—or, rather, someone who fancies you," Karan said with a smile.

"Perhaps."

"By the way, I think you have a visitor," Karan said, pointing to the far end of the platform.

Mahesh craned his neck to look. Aarvi was making her way toward him.

"Aarvi . . ." Although he was outwardly calm, his heart was racing. He was so engulfed in a whole slew of emotions that he didn't know what to do next as they stood silently, gazing at each other.

Karan gently touched his arm. "I think I will leave now," he said, giving Mahesh a big hug and a smile. Karan looked at Aarvi and nodded before leaving.

Turning again, Mahesh saw that Aarvi was only a few steps away. She walked up to Mahesh, still wearing all the henna and makeup from the ceremony the night before. Dressed in white and looking radiant as ever, she seemed out of place in the station with its weary passengers.

"I couldn't let you leave without saying goodbye," she said.

"I am glad you came," Mahesh replied softly.

"Mahesh . . ."

"Yes?"

"I'm sorry about what I said earlier. I don't know what came over me. I wish you had come to the party last night."

"That's all right. You have absolutely nothing to apologize for," Mahesh said.

"Yes, I do," she said, her eyes meeting his.

"Don't worry about it. I shouldn't have been so forthcoming in offering my views on things I know little about."

"No, you absolutely should have. That's what friends are for. If you must know, I never doubted your sincerity, and I know that your intentions were always noble." She moved closer to him.

"It has been a wonderful trip for me, even though I'm sad that we didn't have more time."

"Me too," she whispered.

"I guess that's the way things roll sometimes. You know, Aarvi, I met you in Hari Das's residence on Monday, and we haven't even known each other for a week. But it seems like we have known each other for a long, long time."

"Like old friends?"

"Yes," Mahesh replied, looking at Aarvi with a sad smile. He could see her eyes welling up.

"I guess you are all set for your trip."

"I am."

"Next Saturday, you will be off on another grand adventure," Aarvi mumbled.

"Well, the one this week was pretty grand too, and unforgettable. You will be starting a new chapter as well."

"I will," Aarvi whispered.

"How did you explain coming here at this hour to your parents?"

"I came with my father. He drove me here and is waiting for me in the car outside."

"Oh, please do thank him for me."

Though Mahesh could see the sadness in her eyes, she managed a weak smile. He felt a lump in his throat, desperately wanting to reach out, wrap his arms around her, and let her know how much she meant to him. He held back, not knowing what to do next.

"I have something for you, for your journey."

"You shouldn't have. I love the food on the trains."

"It's not food," Aarvi said, reaching into her bag and pulling out two small books. She handed them to Mahesh.

"What's this?"

"The first one is on the history of Benares. It was written more than three decades ago by a famous local author, and it's a first edition," she said, pointing to the larger of the two books. Mahesh scanned the cover and the back.

"Thank you, and the other one?" he asked, holding up the second book. It looked like a notebook with a hard cover and typewritten pages inside. It didn't quite look like a published book.

"That's from a lesser-known amateur writer in Benares."

"It's yours," Mahesh said, eyes widening in surprise.

"Yes, it's a collection of short stories I've written over the years. No one has ever seen them, much less read them. I have a notebook where I write things down. This one is the first and only typewritten copy. It's yours."

"Oh my God. You must publish these! This is so impressive. I am so proud of you, and you should be so proud of yourself," he said, his heart overflowing with genuine admiration.

Aarvi stared back at him with a bittersweet wistfulness. Just as she opened her mouth to say something, the train horn blew to signal that it would be leaving in a few minutes.

Aarvi turned and gazed into Mahesh's eyes. There was so much they wanted to say to each other. For a moment, time stood still, neither knowing what to say or do next.

"Our short journey has come to an end," Aarvi said, her voice tight.

"I will treasure the books you gave me, but what I will remember most is the wonderful time I had with one of the best people I've ever met," Mahesh said.

There was another blow of the horn, and the train started moving slowly. As they looked toward the front of the train, they could hear the hissing of the coaches inching forward and saw the steam emanating from the wheels. Mahesh turned slightly and started climbing the steps to get into his coach when he felt a hand on his arm.

Aarvi drew him closer and gave him a long embrace. He could feel her hair on his shoulders, her breath on his cheek. Before she let go, she gently whispered into his ear.

"Go well, my dear, dear friend. I hope you succeed in whatever you do. I wish you luck and I wish you happiness," she said.

Before Mahesh could say anything, Aarvi spun and started toward the exit. As he climbed the steps into the slow-moving train, he watched her back as she walked away. She stopped, turning briefly to wave at him. Still standing at the door of the moving train, he waved back at his friend, who wiped a tear with her handkerchief. The train had now picked up speed, and his coach swept past where she was standing. Then she was gone. He strained his neck through the open door, but the train had left the platform and was well on its way.

Mahesh trudged back to his berth and took his seat. His fellow passengers, probably noticing that he looked sad, asked him if he was all right. He smiled and gently nodded.

He looked out the window to get a final glimpse of the river that had defined this city for centuries. The skies were overcast, and it began to rain. He listened to the falling rain patter on the roof of the train. He closed his eyes and tried to sleep. Although he hadn't slept much the night before, he couldn't rest. Slowly, he reached into his bag, brought out the book with Aarvi's typewritten pages, and started to read.

Epilogue

December 1980 in London was no different than any other. However, on this Monday, there was a lull in the driving rain and bitter wind. Although it was still overcast, the streets and sidewalks were bustling with signs of Christmas and New Year's Eve. The lights in the shops and the clamor of people excited for the upcoming winter break brought a warm, festive atmosphere to the vibrant city.

Mahesh's apartment building was located a few blocks from the university. During the last few months, living in London had been both challenging and exciting. He had grown to love the historic city with everything it had to offer. Although the weather had tested him, he had managed reasonably well, making sure that he dressed warmly and always had an umbrella or a light raincoat.

What had really challenged him was the way the PhD program was taught at the university. Unlike what he was used to in India, there was a lot of independent coursework and reading. He was mentally prepared for both, but the volume of work, at times, had been overwhelming. He liked his supervisor, and, being a hard worker, he was gradually adjusting to the pace of the program. The part that thrilled him most was the time he spent with his fellow students from all over the world. The international faculty at his university was only matched by the student body hailing from countries he couldn't even place on a map. He was sharing his apartment with a student from Jamaica and another from Argentina.

This morning, he was waiting for his Jamaican friend, Clive, to get ready so they could walk to the university together. Clive reminded Mahesh of Bharat in many ways. They had a lot in common in their desire to nap for long hours, eat slowly, and joke about everything.

"C'mon, Clive. It's already nine. Hurry up!" Mahesh shouted as he sat at a small kitchen table, helping himself to some tea.

"Ma'ahesh, ma'an!" Clive yelled from his room, his Caribbean accent prominent. "Histo'ory has waited for centuries and is not going anywhere. It can wait for a few more minutes for me to get ready."

That made Mahesh laugh. He picked up his cup and moved to the window overlooking the narrow cobblestone street. Their apartment was on the top floor of the three-story building. As he gazed out the window, he watched the people below go about their daily lives. Looking down toward the street, he saw a postman walking up to the door.

He opened the window and strained his neck, and he saw that the man had left a small package near the door. Mahesh wondered if it was for him. He was expecting a few photos from his parents, who had gone on a family vacation. Being in London meant missing out on those get-togethers. He looked over his shoulder and heard running water in the bathroom. Clive was still getting ready. Mahesh quickly went down the stairs to check what the postman had left.

It was a parcel for him. He brought it back up and read the label. It was from Karan. Mahesh opened it carefully, not wanting to damage anything inside. He sat down and emptied the contents onto the kitchen table.

There was a one-page letter from Karan. He read and reread it. Then his gaze moved to the other item in the envelope. It was a copy of *The Benares Examiner*.

He checked the date; it was from a few weeks ago. Mail from India took almost a week to get to London, and that was when it was sent from one of the major metros, like Delhi, Bombay, or Calcutta. This was from Benares, which meant at least another two or three days. Unlike national dailies, *The Benares Examiner* was a small local daily with only a few pages. Karan had marked up two articles on separate pages.

The first article was on the front page, written by Deepika Roy. While it was a long news story, the gist of it was that the police had solved the death of Devesh Tripathi. Initially, police had treated the death as a result of health complications due to a hit-and-run. After a thorough investigation, it was determined that the accident wasn't random. The professor's nephew and niece-in-law, Laxman and Rani Tripathi, had been questioned and taken into custody by the police following a statement from a lorry driver whom the police were able to locate. The driver was also implicated in the crime.

The investigation, led by Officer Bhanu Dev from the Sarnath Police Station, also uncovered callousness on the part of the doctor who had examined Devesh. Although no formal charges were brought against him, the hospital where he was working had instituted a committee for further disciplinary action. As for the motive, it seemed that Laxman's company was in trouble financially, and he was heavily indebted.

The article went on to say that Devesh had contacted a lawyer to formulate a new will bequeathing most of his assets to someone in Jaunpur. *So, he knew,* Mahesh thought, and that made him smile. In the article, it was mentioned that the police were grateful for the assistance they had received from one Mr. Hari Das and two other members of the public who wished to remain anonymous.

Mahesh then shifted his attention to the second article, which was on the last page. It was about the Sanskriti Bookshop near Assi Ghat in Benares. The bookstore had come up with a novel way of promoting new and upcoming authors. Each month, a few writers would be asked to talk about their books. The store would also invite publishers and members of the public to short book readings and discussions. There were details on how the authors would be selected, which genres would be covered, and that preference would be given to those who hadn't yet been published. It went on to say that the idea was the brainchild of Mrs. Aarvi Kumar, who would be managing the initiative. Finally, it stated that the bookstore would be publishing crossword puzzles in the newspaper each weekend.

Below the article was a large picture of the inside of the bookstore. The photograph showed the neatly arranged bookshelves in the background with some customers and employees behind the counters in the foreground and on one side. On the other side of the photograph was a picture of Aarvi sitting behind a large desk. Although the photograph was a bit grainy, she clearly stood out from everything and everyone else in the picture. *So, she finally got her way and was able to go back to the bookstore after her marriage.* That made Mahesh happy, knowing how much it meant to her.

He reread both articles, and his gaze fell on Aarvi's face in the photograph. He looked carefully, having missed seeing something the first time he had looked at the picture. It was so tiny that it could easily have gone unnoticed. In Aarvi's hand was the small wooden pen that he had given her. That brought a sad smile to Mahesh's face. He set the contents down, placed the envelope back on the kitchen table, and moved to the window to look outside.

The clouds were slowly parting, and the sun was desperately trying to peek through and make its presence felt. He closed his eyes and let his mind wander. He didn't notice that Clive had walked up to him and was standing right next to him. Mahesh was startled when Clive touched his arm. He quickly spun to look at his roommate.

"Now, I know that kind of smile, Ma'ahesh," Clive teased.

"Hmm. How do you know?" Mahesh asked, grinning.

"That kind of smile has to do with a wom'aan. I know it. Am I right or am I right?"

"Hmm," Mahesh said, still smiling.

"See, I was right. One day, you will have to tell me all about it."

"I will," Mahesh said. "One day, I will. But now, my friend, history is waiting for us."

"True."

Mahesh and Clive walked out of their apartment building, stepping onto the street toward their university.

About the Author

Aditya Banerjee grew up in India and moved to Canada in the nineties. He is a graduate of McGill University in Montreal, Canada, and Manipal Institute of Technology in Manipal, India. An avid traveler, he is a history buff and has authored several mysteries and fiction novels. He is the creator of detective Shankar Sen and the author of *Broken Dreams: A Callipur Murder Mystery, Stolen Legacies*, and *Death in the Walled City*. Aditya lives with his family in Canada.

Printed in Great Britain
by Amazon